AGES

Richard William Hershey, Jr.

Star Chamber Press
Burlington, Vermont

ISBN 1448680700

Printed by Star Chamber Press; Burlington, Vermont.
First edition, first printing.

For more information regarding other titles published by Star Chamber Press, please visit *www.starchamberpress.com*

AGES

Richard William Hershey, Jr.

Translator's Introduction

The following text was translated from a manuscript found in Ethiopia, beginning in the Fall of 1977 and concluding in August 2008. The author of the source text is unknown. The glyphs accompanying each segment and pictured on the cover were recreated to accomplish two functions. First, they denote breaks in the source text, where the author presumably suspended inscription for an indefinite amount of time. Second, the images present to the reader examples of the source text itself.

The glyphs pictured were taken from the source matrix, although none involved in the transfer process handled the manuscript or were shown images other than those found in this first edition. (Special thanks to art consultant Maarten van der Poll, for his generous help in rendering the images appearing in this book.)

What we do know for certain about the source text is that it is composed in a language previously unknown to modern scholars. Further, due to the circumstances surrounding its discovery, the source text can be dated to a time well before our base of written history. To provide for the reader the archaeological context in which the source text was discovered, I have included as Appendix 1 a detailed account of its acquisition. It may be beneficial to read Appendix 1 prior to the translated text, but this should be done at the discretion of the reader and by no means does the source require the benefit of such an introduction. Appendix 2 provides explanatory along with translational notes clarifying certain words from the source; however, the text may be read independent of these notes and are my liberty alone, denoting no intention by the author.

In the interest of preserving the safety of the source text

I have chosen to keep my name anonymous. I am aware that many would clamber to study it themselves, but presenting the original manuscript to the public is not possible.

S.I.C.
2009

Segment 1

Chamber

1

Through time and space and spinning dust, its spectral glow for each of us, from churning froth to parched tongue, comes certainly for everyone, an ever less-forgiving friend, come quickly now, for me, the end.

I can't help but hum the tune to this familiar children's song over and over to myself. It's been recited a thousand times before but never meant anything to me before now. Of course, the song is about death. There were many in my world who believed something happens after a person dies, a different type of experience to be had. Perhaps of all people I should know what to expect, but unfortunately this is not the case. I will know all about death in a few days, though, only this time I can't return to tell you about it. You see, this will not be my first death, but will surely be my last.

So as you read the story I'm about to tell, keep this one fact in mind—I'm dead. I died a long time ago, long before your world[1] came into existence. Don't be confused, though. We inhabit the same planet, see the same stars, are likely similar in appearance, but we live in completely different ages[2], different eras in our planet's history. Impossible, you say? Read and you will believe. Now that I think of it, that you're reading this is a wonder in itself; my language and writing system are certainly unknown to your world. I admit, when I was finally shut in here I had lingering doubts that my story would survive to reach you. But you are reading, and that means hope still exists, hope that your world will not suffer as mine has.

The unfortunate truth is that my story does not have a happy conclusion. It's the account of how my world came to an end. Now when I say "came to an end," I don't mean that the planet disintegrated; time still stumbled forward, the sun continued to burn. But the people, the buildings, the cultures that I claim as part of who I am are gone. The things that made up my world have vanished from the planet. The cultures were abandoned in favor of pleasures and greed, the buildings have all burned and crumbled, and the people are almost all dead. Indeed, an entire planet's population and everything we accomplished have been wiped away, a great purging. The worst part is, we've chosen this as our fate.

You're right to wonder how a dead person can tell a story. Of course, as I write this I'm not yet passed, but I will be in a matter of days. There's absolutely no saving me, no chance of survival. Outside the air is poison to breath, water rises vile beyond use, and fire drips from the blackened sky, torching everything it touches. Still, you must be wondering how these words have survived when my entire world has been destroyed. Please allow me to explain.

At the moment I am sitting in a room located deep beneath the ground, alone, and in complete darkness[3]. This chamber was constructed to withstand natural disasters and stay in tact for a very long time, so it's obviously served its function well. But I'm not here simply to die, I came here to complete my final duty. I can't take credit for the chamber or even the idea of chronicling the details of our demise; a wise man from my world instructed me to come here and I listened. The chamber merely keeps me alive a few days longer so I can write[4] as the land above me burns.

It is important you know who I was, so I must take a moment to introduce myself and my world. I was one of the most recognized people on earth during my age; everyone knew me. I was a leader at the highest level, a Prophet-King[5], in charge of the fate of almost every person on earth. It was my words the people trusted, my decisions they accepted, and my advice they took. I really never sought this high position, it happened on its own, but I also did not reject it when it became my duty. In a way, though, I wish I had, if for no other reason than to spare the People. They trusted me; they trusted me and I failed them.

Thinking back, my younger years seem insignificant compared to what Aigonz had planned. I was born into royalty, which automatically qualified me as a Noble. There were many other Nobles and together we formed a kind of ruling class over those who didn't have the advantage of aristocratic birth. As a child I had access to the finest education and never wanted for anything. The People[6] labored day and night, but we Nobles never worked with our hands. Because of my status I had the privilege of traveling far and wide. I saw firsthand the kinds of things others only heard about. I was able to travel across the ocean, to see the great ice-shelves[7] towering above the water and stretching forever over the land. I glided alongside every animal and mingled with every type of person on earth, finding friends everywhere I went with hardly a moment of discontent; every person, that is, except those we called the Forgotten People. I wouldn't meet them until much too late.

After my time spent traveling, I went into service for the government[8], as did all Nobles, working as a low level scribe[9] and leading a comfortable and relatively anonymous life. You see, in my world, most of the rule-makers were born into their position, but the only birthright granted the People was censure. My society was structured so there were always a large number of people with no power and a few who made all the social decisions. Nobles decided what was right and what was wrong, who had to work and who didn't, who ate and who starved. Because these political[10] powers didn't earn their positions, they were almost always unqualified to rule. Further, Nobles lived a life of such luxury and excess that they cared little about the People's needs. Consequently, they made a practice of twisting social policy to benefit themselves and their families while others suffered from this contrived inequity.

But because the system of rule was so detached from the needs of the People, few of them knew anything about their rulers, and those who did know how things were run were powerless to stop it and so broken by fear they didn't have the will to fight for their freedom. Early in the history of my world, Nobles decided that the People should never be more than unshackled slaves. You see, they designed a system to keep the People under control, a system of currency[11]. This was a sort of glorified trade system where vouchers[12] were issued and controlled by the aristocracy, who determined their worth and their purchasing power.

In its infancy, the currency system was touted as a safe, revolutionary breakthrough for the advancement of equality in our world. It was dressed up to seem very attractive to the People, who thought it was their chance to gain a little ground on the Nobles, to enjoy just a humble portion of the comforts my world had developed but not equally shared. What they didn't realize is that the system was designed to secretly rob them of their vouchers and, consequently, their freedom.

It is the case that, in my world, many years before I was born, people would exchange items like food and clothing for certain stones, pieces of hardened minerals, and other such natural objects[13]. Some of these natural objects had practical uses and others didn't. For example, we had a mineral that could burn for hours, providing heat in the cold areas and during the cold times[14]. We also had plants that would accomplish the same function, and additionally could be used for building shelters and tools. These objects were collected by people and traded with no further obligation.

But somewhere along the way, people, perhaps out of convenience or perhaps by coercion, replaced the exchange of natural objects with the exchange of vouchers. Valuable natural objects were stored in a central location and a voucher was issued by the person or people holding the objects, detailing how much was stored and how much could be demanded if the voucher was redeemed. The vouchers were then exchanged for food, clothing, or shelter because they had the same value as the natural objects they represented.

This seemed like a very useful and safe way to trade and so was accepted by more and more people over time. Soon, natural objects were rarely used to trade and instead vouchers were present everywhere, exchanged for everything and given as reward for work. Some people began to collect their vouchers and hold them, unredeemed. Others began searching the world, looking for natural objects that could be exchanged for vouchers. Eventually some people began amassing large amounts while others had very few and little chance of gaining more.

Those with large stores of vouchers realized they could be lent to others who needed them with the promise they would be returned to the original owner, plus extra as a reward for the loan. For many people, this meant that they could obtain items they needed but couldn't afford, provided the vouchers were returned with a little extra compensation.

But some people in my world were very tricky. Those holding natural objects realized they could simply create more vouchers without increasing their cache of natural objects and no one would ever know. And this is what they did, creating vouchers that actually had no worth but using them as if they did. All of a sudden, huge amounts of vouchers were available to be borrowed, all of which had to be returned with interest[15].

The end result of this process was that those who created false vouchers would be given back legitimate vouchers as interest. So basically, Nobles were robbing the People of their natural objects because they lied about their vouchers being legitimate. This enabled lenders to amass huge stores of wealth[16], all based on deception. Their vouchers couldn't be redeemed for natural objects because those natural objects weren't available; they didn't even exist, but were invented for the purpose of thievery.

This gave way to a more sophisticated and streamlined system, in which real currency was replaced by a sort of ineffable collection of units[17], abstract instances of purchasing power that were counted and held by a Central Distributor and could be added to or deducted from. People used their units to acquire food, land and other material items they needed as basic necessities of life, just as they'd used vouchers in the past. Units were constantly being traded back and forth, establishing an intricate web-flow in which they gained and lost value. What the People didn't realize was that as the Central Distributor held their currency, it was quietly taking units away and adding them to the wealth of those in control of the institution, the Nobles. But the People were so uninformed that they didn't notice what happened to their unit collection as long as their immediate needs were met.

My new friend, this is the condition I was born into. By the time I appeared on earth[18], most people spent their lives trying to gain more vouchers, only to have them taken away by lenders. Voucher/unit collecting became a driving force in many people's lives, including my own. Soon, the largest collections meant the most power, even among the Nobles. I admit I entered this world already in a situation that made it easy for me to collect vouchers, as my kin had vigorously done so before I appeared, and before my resurrection I spent almost all of my time Collecting.

As I said, most people in my world genuinely had no idea they were slaves[19] to the elite, for it was the type of slavery born of deception. I had a privileged knowledge of the system, a Noble's view, but even this was mired in lies and clever deception. It was only through my relationship with one man that everything became clear to me, though clarity was not his intention. His name was Edensaw Megedagik Tasapainottaa[20], and he is dead now too, or at least as dead as I'll be in a few days. Eden was a man of science, a man respected the world over. Eden was also a great deceiver, a nefarious and calculating manipulator; I trusted him and he lied to me.

If there was one other person in my world who was as recognized as myself, it was Eden. During our time together I admit I knew little about his childhood. He never talked about it and I never asked. In my world, Nobles communicated on a generally superficial level, so details about a person's life might never come to light. Eden was very closed about his past, and though our relationship ventured far into the realm of intimacy he never shared with me even the most basic information about himself. Of course, I told Eden everything about myself whether he wanted to hear it or not, and he listened with seeming patience. I asked him once to tell me about his parents, about his upbringing. He became suddenly withdrawn and left the room without so much as a word of explanation. Now in my world, it was a breach of etiquette for a Noble to ask another Noble about her personal life. Eden and I grew so close, though, that sharing these details seemed only natural.

But he would have no part in revealing his past and I never asked again. Of course, I found out later why it was such a guarded secret, but by then it didn't matter anyway. In my opinion, Eden had one purpose, one goal in life, and that was to become great. And he was great. Eden introduced technologies the likes of which had never been seen in my world. He brought together Nobles from every background and was loved and trusted by all, including me. But Eden was evil[21], evil to his very center. Unfortunately for my world, I found this out when it was already too late.

But for now, my head is spinning from the events that have landed me in this room. My hand still trembles from fear and fatigue. The smell of burning life lingers in my hair, on my clothes, and the memory of a world brought to its knees by its own devices dances violently in my mind. And above it all, high above, sings a child, dancing wildly with her friends, hands joined, gleefully splashing in filth, all reciting their morbid prophecy: *Through time and space and spinning dust, its spectral glow for each of us, from churning froth to parched tongue, comes certainly for everyone, an ever less-forgiving friend, come quickly now, for me, the end.*

I must rest for a moment, but I urge you, read my story. I wrote it for you. It has survived a thousand lifetimes to appear before your eyes. Join me in remembering what your world has certainly forgotten. After all, this is the story of the end of an age, the end of all ages.

Segment 2

Resurrection

2

It seems to me we're born with few fears, being alone or hungry maybe, but those fears we develop as we age were likely given to us by someone else. My grandmother always used to say "A child will forever be a child," and I think she meant that, no matter what point in time, no matter where on earth, children will act in similar ways. I used to point this out to my followers. Children demonstrate for us a more fundamental type of human than we become later in life, I told them. I always wondered, what's it like to be an infant[1]? How do they experience things, or more so, how do infants remember things? Until I had a language to use, I don't recall a thing.

I must say, though, that in my life I never had much to fear. I always acted according to my passions and left fear for when it was truly needed, though laying here in this blackness, wheezing from the dust, the earth around me trembling in birth-pains[2], I wonder if perhaps fear would have saved us. There were some people in my world who used fear to control the actions of others, though that was never my method of communicating. But there was one time that I was very afraid, afraid for my life, and I had good reason to be, because my life was taken from me. As I mentioned before, when I succumb (to the next place), it will not be the first time I've died.

The last time I wrote I explained to you a system of currency that pervaded my world. Well, that system not only pervaded my world but also myself as well. You see, after my stint as a government scribe I decided to pass time as a Collector[3]. I spent my days figuring out ways to increase the number of units in my collection; as a pass-time of many Nobles this was regarded as a highly respectable position.

Because of my Noble birth I had access to the

knowledge and opinion of the finest Collectors of any age. These Collectors could increase their amounts in huge sums, all by way of Noble Decree or public terror. I found Collection to be a most comfortable way of life, one that offered huge advantages in my world. I had everything a person could ever need or wish for. It was as fine a life as could be, and it was really all I knew. But one day that life came to an abrupt end.

I was returning from a long day's duties, and was awaiting my home and rest. I stood on the Beltway[4] and was whisked along, with many others around me jostling in their fixtures. I remember staring at the squat metal city buildings that rushed by beneath me, creating a pattern of light and dark that looked like nothing in particular yet something from which I couldn't look away. The Beltway would sometimes cause me to slip into this enchanted state, so deep that I was often oblivious to those around me. In fact, there were instances on the Beltway when I became so engrossed in my own reverie it seemed like no time at all had passed before I was home.

But that particular day, something caught my eye that broke me from my trance. I was swaying peacefully as always when off to my right, mixed in among the other people, I couldn't help but notice a nervous man swaying his body back and forth and staring in my direction. Curious, I turned to look at the man. To my surprise, he was staring directly at me. As our gazes connected my curiosity vanished.

His eyes were black like Lawurl[5] and gleamed with a hideous darkness, the sight of which sent my body spiraling into tremors of fear. Realizing he was discovered he jerked his head away, as if to hide from me by averting his gaze, and began to rock himself, so violently that the people around him squirmed in their fixtures, moving as far away from the man as they could. I turned my head and looked back at the floor as if he would cease to exist if I couldn't see him.

The Beltway stuttered to a stop and I stared at him from the sides of my eyes. I watched the man reach for his release cord, run out onto the platforms and jump into a Ground-Finder[6]. Relief washed over me as he left, negativity flowing in waves from my body. 'He is gone now, I can relax,' I reassured myself.

The farther we journeyed from the man the calmer I became, and by the time I exited the Beltway I had all but forgotten the incident. I settled into the Ground-Finder and peered at the earth below through the grid of metal at my feet. The doors clanked behind me and the engines hummed to life. 'It will take them a moment to warm up,' I thought. But as I stood waiting a sudden paranoia fell over me, as if a human presence lurked very close but just out of sight. I glanced around nervously. I was alone and in almost complete darkness, the lights on the machine remaining quite dim until it started to move.

"There's no one here but me!" I exclaimed aloud, attempting in vain to reassure myself. But even as the words escaped my mouth I felt a figure materialize from the shadows in front of me, approaching very slowly and shrouded in darkness. Electricity shot through my body, every inch of skin tensing. I stood still as death, hoping that what I saw was only an illusion[7]. 'This isn't real,' I repeated over and over, 'your eyes are playing tricks on you in the dark.'

But I couldn't shake the feeling I was not alone. "Hello?! Who's there?!" I choked, my voice quivering nervously. Suddenly, the Ground-Finder shook into motion and the lights blazed. When they did I recoiled at what I saw, my back pressed against the wall of the Ground-Finder. "It's you...from the...!" I gasped aloud, my breath fleeting, my body urging fluids to be evacuated.

The man from the Beltway walked slowly toward me from the opposite end of the Ground-Finder. His glistening hair hung limp in front of his face in strands, dripping and soaked with sweat. He had a long dirty beard tangled in clumps and stuck to his head as though smeared with wax. His eyes were sunken into his pale face in dark black circle, the lids drooping to form small black slits, like he was asleep. A piercing-needle trembled in his left hand.

He muttered to himself, repeating the same thing over and over, "Aigonz do your work through me. Aigonz do your work through me."

"What do you want from me?" I screamed at him as he approached. Instead of answering he lunged at me and, using both hands, sunk the needle deep into my chest. I stared into his vacant face, desperately gripping his wrist in a useless attempt to remove the needle as he slowly plunged the contents into my body.

He stepped back. We were face to face, the needle still hanging out of my chest as I stood motionless from shock, feeling nothing. His eyes opened and we connected for a moment. I remember the look in those eyes, like nothing I'd ever seen. They were deep, black pits, emitting a remarkable shining quality, but also a disconnection, as if this man was perfectly cognoscente of his duty but consciously unaware of his actions. The jolting of the Ground-Finder broke our connection and, as quickly as he'd attacked, he turned and ran, leaving the empty needle for me to remove. I collapsed to the floor and prepared to die. Poison crept slowly through me, leaving the warmth of death everywhere it traveled.

I'll never forget the feeling of those moments before my death[8]. My eyes no longer caught the light, my ears plugged and refused to gather sound, and I could not feel with my hands. Yet despite these deprivations I experienced only bliss, a feeling of immense peace and ecstatic joy. My body glowed; it felt vibrant, radiant, sharp, as if for the first time, in death, I was truly alive.

But this type of living was done outside of my body, outside of my hands and eyes and ears. I felt everything and nothing all at once. I heard my labored breath grind to a halt, as if it had all along been merely a musician performing for my amusement. My heart announced to me its intention to stop and I watched as it failed, relieved of its duties[9]. I felt myself rushing, as if I was drawing upward at an incredible speed, leaving my body behind as an afterthought, a distant memory. I approached an equilibrium when suddenly I felt myself becoming impressed with knowledge, like shadows of an undiscovered past, glaciers of forgotten truth.

In a way, I felt as though I was being restored, like I'd lost a part of myself that I was just then recovering. I remembered events from my life, but I felt them rather than thought them. I remembered events from lives that weren't even my own, things I'd never experienced but felt as though I had. I remember this state as an indescribable beauty, a fullness, a completion of myself; thinking back now it's possible this was the feeling of pure positive Viria, or at least the removal of the negative.

Then, just as quickly as it began, I felt myself rushing back. My body slowly regained feeling as the blissful state faded, giving way to pangs of physical pain. The next thing I remember, I gasped aloud, sat bolt upright and threw my eyes open. A harsh light shone from above me. I lay back and squinted at the light, breathing deep as air flooded into my starving lungs. Faces circled around me, peering into my line of sight. These were doctors.

"What happened?" I muttered, propping myself up on my elbows, my head tumbling in fits of confusion.

"You have been dead for two hours[10]," one of the faces answered.

"That's impossible," I said. "It's been no time at all." Truly, it felt as though I'd just fallen to the floor of the Ground-

Finder a moment ago. Then, my wits returning, I remembered the horrible man, the piercing-needle, and fell back into the bed, deep into unconsciousness.

I awoke from my coma days later to a different world, or at least a different way of looking at things. It was as if I saw through new eyes, felt with new fingers. My mind swirled with new information, new impressions. My person[11] had changed. No more was the old life, the old way of thinking. I couldn't remember my name or my pass-time[12] or anything else that would have connected me with my old way, nor did I care to. When my Care-Workers found me I'd risen from my bed and gone out onto the balcony. The warm breeze caressed my skin, exciting every hair to taste the beauty of life, to drink the sunlight—I started to feel, really feel, for the first time.

This was a living I'd never done before. In a way, it was a compliment to the feeling of death, which by that point I fully remembered and understood. But this was the experience of life, not death, and it had a sweetness all its own.

"You must come inside. You have been very ill and need rest," said a voice from behind me. A kind woman put her hand on my arm and led me back to my room.

I looked up at her as I lay down. She was smiling, a bright light behind her obscuring her face. She didn't speak, but rubbed my hand gently. As she did, floods of my old life came back. Memories of my childhood, of family, of Collecting. I squinted at her and smiled back. She turned and left me to sleep, to dream the first dreams of my new life.

As you can imagine I spent the next few weeks recovering. Upon inquiring as to his whereabouts I was told the man who attacked me had been found and was being safely held in an institution for those with similar mental abnormalities[13]. I was also informed that, before my recovery and subsequent coma, I'd been dead for at least two hours, declared beyond hope. But as I lay in the corpse-room, apart from any observable cause, I began taking shallow breaths followed by eye flutters and facial movements. The doctor on duty noticed one of his corpses coming back to life and sounded the alarm just as my heart began beating unaided and my brain activity slowly returned to normal. Doctors shouted for others to come see and they swarmed into the room and crowded around me, astonished by a person returning from the dead.

And indeed, that's what happened to me. A resurrection of my body, completely unaided and unprovoked. I can't explain it nor have I ever tried to. But from that point on I knew my duty. I was informed that during my coma I was continually uttering verses[14], all of which were recorded and given to me. As I listened to my own voice gushing with enthusiasm, making statements about Reality, about the way things really are, I was amazed to find that all of what I heard myself say I also felt as truth inside me. Like a painting on the wall or a shadow burned into the eye, it whispered through me and permeated my flesh. So when I left the Healing-Place, I took those recordings with me and wrote them down feverishly, copied with absolute care to accurately preserve every word.

From those verses I would eventually distribute a great treatise on the nature of Reality, but this would be simply a stepping stone toward world-recognition. I began to tour the Regions, meeting the People and forging relationships with other Nobles. In fact, after my first tour alone I counted among my followers at least half of the population of the earth, including Nobles from all 10 Regions[15]. The only group not represented were the Forgotten People; they were not in need of a teacher.

I traveled for years, and my following increased to the

point that a religion developed around me and my teachings. At first, I resisted the idea of being a prophet. I didn't consider myself worthy of leading such a huge amount of people, afraid of doing the wrong thing, of leading them astray. But the more attention I received, the easier it was for me to slip into the role; it felt as though I'd been selected and had no other choice but to accept.

Now because of my new position of prominence and my advantage of Noble birth, I was given access to the great leaders of my age. When my public following grew to the point that it could no longer be ignored by the law-makers, I yet again toured the earth, this time meeting with leaders in each Region and discussing how I might help improve the situation of my fellow people, for many suffered under the weight of debt and indenture. As I traveled, I was accompanied by throngs of followers, hoping to catch a glimpse of me.

It was during one of those political tours that I first met Eden. He and I were both in attendance at a Gathering of the 10, where I was invited to assist the Governors in creating a Fear. Eden was receiving much attention for a new design, then still in the conceptual phase, which he claimed was capable of providing virtually limitless energy[16] to be harnessed and used for whatever purpose we saw fit.

Before Eden's design, energy was provided in many different forms, but all had flaws hindering their usefulness. Eden's theory would make it possible for all 10 Regions to power their cities, without shut-down periods or blackouts. I remember some Governors at the meeting were expressing their concern about how safe the design was. This type of power has never been used before, they argued, and we do not yet know if there will be any negative repercussions. Eden, as he would do many times after, assured them that the plans were sound. In fact, he said it was against the very properties, the very nature of the system for anything negative to happen as a result of his design.

Eden was like that. He had a certain way that enabled him to convince anyone of anything. He just always made sense. Other people in my world would sometimes become confused or emotional and confound their thoughts, or simply remain silent, unable to articulate what they felt but desperately wanted to communicate. But Eden would always say the best possible thing at the best possible time. He had charm enough to befit a prince, an air of confidence that commanded respect, and the words of the universe itself when describing his thoughts. He was a thinker, an artisan, a scientist, and the person everyone wanted to spend time with; especially me.

Segment 3

Edensaw Megedagik Tasapainottaa

3

I'm actually quite comfortable here in my tomb. I don't fear death, in fact I like the thought of returning to that blissful state, but before I can enjoy the next place I must again endure the passage[1] into death, pay the price of admission[2]. For some the price is cheap—people who vanished from Amaia were dead before they knew what happened, and surely felt no pain. But for others, passage is costly. There were some in my world who lived to endure a costly end. You see, we enforced a strict code of laws that, when violated, held a severe penalty. Each citizen was given one reprieve, one unpunished violation against society. But if a person was found to be in violation for a second time, she would be confined to the cages[3].

The cages were located in the center of every city and housed all offenders, from those committing petty crimes to the most heinous evils ever conceived. All were placed together in a series of confinement cubes, four or five to a cube, and suspended high above the People. According to the law, punishment provided no differentiation between a thief and a speaker-against-the-government, a non-worker and a murderer. All who committed second offenses were placed in the cages for the duration of their sentence, some for only a few years, others until they were dead. The cages were flushed every so often and food was dropped once a day through holes in the top, but despite these concessions the cages were a difficult punishment to endure and many who entered never returned.

For these people, admission to death was costly; it was painful, filled with sorrow, and devoid of hope. Here in my tomb I am reminded of the cages, although my situation is not quite so desperate. It's true I'll be dead in a very short time. It's true I'll suffer; even now, after only a short time in this place my tongue cries for water, my body rumbles for food. But unlike those in the cages, I'll succumb with the knowledge of Reality, knowledge of the true nature of things, and the duty of passing this knowledge to you. The story of my world is the story of all worlds, from the very first to yours. You may not have cages or vouchers or Amaia in your world, but you do have people, and people have choices.

Eden was a person who believed he made the right choices, and as I know now, for him his choices were good. Even after all this time[4], I remember our first meeting as if it were only moments ago. I was concluding a grand tour of the Regions, landing me in the capital and my home region of Nyanga[5] for a Gathering of the 10, where a crisis was being sold[6] to the People.

Now, creating fear for the People was no great surprise, especially considering my past as a Collector. You see, it happened in my world that all the Governors started working together to intertwine their Region's units, creating a single unified system of currency overseen by the Central Distributor. Although the merging of all 10 economies under a single currency system was a recent occurrence, there'd always been enough communication between the Regions to ensure that what affected one Region could affect others.

One of the easiest ways to increase Collections was to create an environment of fear surrounding people's units and the cost of goods. When people became afraid of losing their collection they were more likely to approve of decisions made by a Governor[7]. This could work to the benefit of any Governor who desired a certain agenda be passed. The strategy was that a Governor or someone within her inner circle would create rumors throughout her Region, or possibly in another Region, telling the people their collection of units was in jeopardy of being lost or rendered worthless. The people would cry out to the Governor that they needed her help, and the Governor would emerge with a new plan to restore public faith in the value of their units. This new plan always involved the people surrendering more control of their units to the Governor, and so in essence the Governor and her inner circle would completely control the value of the units in that Region, as well as the infrastructure intended to be publicly owned.

Remember that, even before the Regions joined under one currency, the web-flow of units affected more than just one Region at a time. This meant that a Governor of one Region could create-the-Fear[8] in her own Region with the intention of affecting another. Thus, one Governor could commission another to create-the-Fear and they both would profit by selling a crisis. This type of thing happened all the time in my world and the Nobles knew it was nothing to be alarmed by. But selling a crisis required the cooperation of the Governors, so they would all meet and discuss the most profitable course of action. It was under these circumstances that I first met Eden.

As I said I was concluding a tour of the Regions when I returned to the place I called my home, the great Region of Nyanga. During the talks it was proposed that a Fear be created concerning the production of energy. While the discussion centered on maximizing profit for the Nobles, it also brought to consideration a new theory of energy production. It was said a great man of science discovered a means by which power could be generated and transferred in an extremely efficient way. This meant that the old way of producing energy, where most of the power generated was lost during transfer, could be replaced. This also meant that the Regions would have virtually unlimited power at their immediate disposal.

Shortly after my arrival, the Governor of Nyanga, Governor Hiru, informed me excitedly that the man responsible for this amazing achievement was in Nyanga and had heard of me. Further, said Hiru, the scientist would very much like to meet me and discuss the future of the Regions. I thought it somewhat presumptuous that this scientist considered himself to have so much influence, and although I admit his ideas were fascinating I regarded him to be no more than a person of intelligence, not quite worthy of a political position.

Our meeting was arranged to be held in the Governor's rooms, private chambers reserved for receiving dignitaries and other Governors. To gaze beyond the doors at the crimson tapestries gently swaying, brushing against the glowing yellow walls, was an honor in itself, and to have an arranged meeting in the Governor's rooms meant you were a person possessing the highest power. My thoughts were elsewhere, however, on that particular day. My Regional tour had brought many concerns to my mind and I was hardly interested in the rooms, which I had seen a number of times before, or the person I was about to meet. But as I approached the gilded archways my focus shifted and I prepared myself for the meeting, shaking off my lingering concerns and clearing my mind to connect with a new person.

I walked into the Governor's rooms to a small group of people crowded around a central figure, gathered so close they appeared to be a single mass of bodies. The rooms had high ceilings completely covered in gold and walls decorated with life-size pictorials of the conquering of the Regions, the creation of the first great city, and other important events in my world's history. Every Governor had her own rooms and each was decorated in a similar fashion. What was unique about these particular rooms was that the decoration included a depiction of the Forgotten People begging to be included in the planning of Nyanga, only to be ignored and exiled in the process. I've always thought it odd that the mural showed history in this way, since I always felt the Forgotten People made a choice to distance themselves from the early cities and remained intentionally separate from the people of my world.

But it was beneath this mural that I found the group conversing excitedly with a tall man, dark skinned and wonderfully handsome. He was wearing the costume of a Noble person, meters[9] of brightly colored fabrics wrapped in the intricate fashion of Nobility. His face was smiling down at those who vied for his attention and he seemed to answer their questions with great enthusiasm. As I approached the group, our eyes met and I assumed a polite grin. He interrupted the passionate conversation and broke from the group, walking across the room to greet me.

Even before we spoke I was wholly attracted to him. His smile was white and broad and his gait confident. But his eyes were the ultimate captors of my affection. They were the color of the clearest sky, the brightest blue against the dark of his skin, a contrast not often seen in my world but highly regarded as the pinnacle of beauty. We drew close and I immediately felt his presence overwhelm me, a sweeping-surge of warmth across my face and down my arms. The cares of the tour disappeared as we joined in a warm embrace, entwining our fingers and performing the usual greeting.

He never broke his gaze during the formalities and I remember, for the first time since the onset of my career as a world-figure, I felt like a servant, a student in the arms of a learned master. As the formalities concluded we remained joined, staring into one another's eyes. I felt like he could see right through me, right into my soul[10], past the figure of flesh and garments others knew. I was at a loss for words and, like a child, stood waiting for him to take the lead. He began in a controlled, clear voice that boomed like thunder but held all the gentleness of soft rain.

"Hello. We've never met but we are meeting now. My name is Edensaw and I have heard much about you. It is an immense pleasure to join faces with you[11]."

"It is indeed a pleasure, Edensaw," I replied, composing

myself, trying to regain my center. "I must say I have been told a great many things about your accomplishments in the field of science. They tell me you have discovered a way to produce more energy than we have ever dreamed possible."

"This is true," he said, "although my accomplishments will extend far past the field of science. These advances are beneficial not only to the Governors but to the People as well; everyone's life will become much more enjoyable." His eyes sparkled as he spoke and I found myself entranced by his musical voice. He laughed and said, "But let's not talk about science right now. There is much time for that."

"Indeed. Tell me Edensaw, why do you meet with Governors and Nobles? Are you of Noble birth?" I asked.

"Nobility is purchased, not inherited, my friend," he answered confidently. "My birth is not a Noble one but my intentions for the Regions are highly beneficent. This is why I drape myself in the cloth of a Noble; I have become Noble by my own virtues." He seemed very confident of his status as he spoke. It was an odd thing to be classified as Noble in my world if one was not born into Nobility. There were few instances of a person being accepted into the aristocracy from outside, but it did happen sometimes. Obviously, Eden had proven himself one of us and was now enjoying the benefits.

"Well it certainly is a pleasure to welcome you into our fold," I said. "The merit of your actions has brought you far, and will continue to carry you, I trust, to the fulfillment of your desires."

"I know it will be so," he replied.

I continued, "So you have requested a meeting with me and I have obliged. Tell me, Edensaw, what do you need from me?"

"I need nothing more than your friendship and your confidence. There are a great many things I wish to accomplish. I have watched your career for some time and decided you will be a great help to me in realizing my plans for the world." His voice licked and soothed my ears, and as he spoke I felt love for this man swelling inside me.

I suddenly realized we were surrounded by people who'd previously melted into the periphery. I also realized Eden and I were still enmeshed in our greeting posture. Embarrassed, I released his hands and started back, apologizing nervously for stepping on the feet of those who crowded close to witness our meeting.

"Perhaps we may continue our conversation in the Governor's private garden, with all respect to our company." Eden turned to the onlookers and excused us both. We joined arms and walked slowly toward the gardens, where we could talk with more privacy.

As we walked, I looked up at Eden and clung to his arm. So strong, well muscled under his robes, I thought. Not typical of a Noble man, being strong and fit. Most Nobles lived a life of complete isolation from work and physical effort, resulting in soft and shapeless bodies. But Eden was a different type of Noble, sculpted from hard work, strong in body and mind. It was not normal for me to be so taken by a person at first meeting, or indeed at all, as I was typically the one receiving all the attention. But I clung to every word he spoke.

As we made our way past the servant's quarters and the Great Hall we exchanged more pleasantries, but the content of these words I cannot recall, so enthralled was I with my new friend. We glided down the shining-stair and into the garden itself, where we were finally alone and could speak freely, without airs.

The Governor's garden was one of the most beautiful places in the Region, kept with the utmost care by a host of servants. Past the shining-stair was a floor that shimmered like ice, but was in reality highly-polished stone. I recall the familiar sound of our shoes clanking on this surface, resounding throughout the Great Hall behind us and disappearing into an explosion of plant life greeting our arrival in the garden. The floor-of-ice gave way to a beautiful green courtyard, perhaps 217 Redetrad[12] around, flanked on all sides by walls of brightly colored flowers and verdure, the scent delicious. Within the immense courtyard were a number of different areas where Nobles could lounge or be entertained, depending on the spot. One area had a number of different pools, stepped so as to pour warm water from one pool to the other, creating a pleasant sound and a cloudy mist that rose from their swirling shallows. Another area had tree-houses so large they could accommodate a large group of Nobles, offering refreshment facilities and the like.

Eden and I walked through the courtyard, arm in arm, enjoying each other's silence in the beauty of the garden. We drifted over to a remote corner, a walled off area covered in green vegetation and likely as old as the Governor's palace itself. There, built into the walls and covered in foliage, we found comfortable couches beneath a pleasant shade, the perfect setting for what was to come. Eden fell into the couches and lounged lazily and across from him I did the same, our bodies nearly disappearing into the green walls. He pulled from his robes a small metal container, gleaming in his dark hand. He removed the top and took a long drink, leaning back with a satisfied grin, his face smooth and relaxed as he reclined.

After a moment, Eden broke our silence. "A lovely spot...the Governor certainly lives a life of luxury," he said whimsically, stroking the branches of the Dheal[13] tree that lightly brushed his shoulder and canopied our conference.

"It's true," I answered. "When the weather turns cold it is more beautiful still."

"But something beautiful to you may not be so to me,"

he mused. "How do I know you will not think me a bore when I say that cold weather is frightful and uncomfortable at best? Will you still be my friend?" His eyes sparkled playfully in the mid-day sun and I admit that, at that moment, he was irresistible to me; I'm sure he knew it, too.

"I would think you a man of your word and that would be good enough for me," I managed, caught off guard when I realized I wasn't listening to what he was saying, so lost was I in my burgeoning passions.

"And a man of his word will be truthful no matter what? Even if it might cost him?"

I laughed, "Perhaps so, but what cost is too high when truth is at stake?" We looked at each other quietly for a moment, taking each other in. Finally, Eden gave his head a slight shake, as if to break himself from some kind of dream-state[14].

"But this is not why I have requested your company." Eden smiled at me and leaned closer. In a soft voice he said, "I have a great plan, a plan only you can help me fulfill."

I was intrigued but at the same time a bit guarded. Everything inside me told me to listen to him, but we had to be better acquainted before I would agree to anything. Still, I was immediately trusting of him and I knew in my heart it was good for me to listen to what he had to say. I decided to proceed with an optimistic caution. Eden leaned back into his couch and took another drink from his flask. He swirled the liquid in his mouth and swallowed slowly, as if to savor every moment the stuff was on his tongue. "Care to try a sample of my newest recipe?" he said, offering me the flask. I took it and held the container up to my nose.

"What is it?" I asked, cringing at the smell that wafted from the opening.

"Another benefit of power, my friend. It requires large amounts of energy to produce, but is well worth the effort.

'The Refreshment of the Nobles,' I have named it to others. Many in the Nobility have proclaimed it the greatest human accomplishment yet achieved," he said with a laugh.

I smiled, "Well, at the risk of poor manners I must decline. The smell is one that my nose refuses to enjoy, I'm afraid, and any further indulgence is therefore impossible." I handed the flask back to Eden, who replaced the top and returned it to his robes.

"But indulgences aside, my new friend, what is your plan and how may I be of assistance?" I asked.

Eden leaned forward, his elbows on his thighs, and touched his fingers together. "My plan is a simple one," he began, a look of excitement glistening in his eyes. "I envision a future where all Regions are unified under a single rule, a future where units are no longer needed to enjoy a comfortable life, and one that brings equality to all people, every class, where the People can live like Nobles." I was impressed by what he said and listened with rapt attention.

He continued, "As you know, there is much corruption among the Regions. Governors even have the power to effect the unit collections of a large number of people in Regions completely apart from their own."

"Yes, I am aware of this crime," I agreed.

"These corrupt Governors are increasing their collections while the People are suffering under the weight of debt."

I nodded, "I know what you say is true."

"It is impossible for the Governors to keep each other in line because they are all involved in making and enforcing the laws for their own Region. They are immune to punishment because they themselves are the law. They will never find themselves stuffed and swinging."

I laughed softly, "No, they will not endure punishment." And it was true. I had spent much time interacting with all the

Governors and knew Eden was right. There is no law for those who enforce the law. Who can judge the judges[15]? Governors did what they liked, when they liked, and no one could tell them to do otherwise. Governors stole, killed, distorted, all to their own benefit. I began to wonder, why had we let this go on for so long without protesting?

As if he'd been reading my thoughts, Eden spoke, "The People don't even know this is happening. They are blinded by what they're told is the reality of their Region. All a Governor needs to do is declare that units are needed to complete some phony social project, and the People surrender the requested units without complaint. Further, if the People do not comply they are eligible for punishment. So they are without options. They must do as they are told. Because they have surrendered so many units to illegitimate causes, they are left with insufficient collections to support their daily activities. So they must borrow units from the Central Distributer, units which must be returned with interest. Of course, as you and I both know, the Central Distributer is controlled by officials answering to a single power—the 10 Governors. Thus, the Governors take their own people's units, forcing them to borrow more units, and gaining still more on the interest incurred."

"Yes, it is a tangled and negative system," I answered. "But it is a new system, only since the economic unification of the Regions has it been in place. It has helped stabilize the volatility that was once present as a result of the use of different Regional unit types."

"It seems to be so, I agree, but this is not true. With a single currency, the Governors can manipulate the system however they please, regardless of the condition of the People."

"And what do you propose will cure this? Rule by a single person, one to whose decree all must submit?" Even as

43

I was saying these words I felt it was impossible. How could one person be trusted to decide the fate of the entire world, to guide and lead in a benevolent way?

"Single rule is the only answer, so long as the person in charge is wholly good and operates with only the best interest of the People in mind," Eden sighed, wiping his forehead with his hand in a gesture of resignation.

"So who do you suggest ascends to such a lofty position?" I was sure he would say himself. This whole conversation had been a set-up to gain my support for him becoming King, I thought.

He grinned, "Why, isn't it clear? That person is you." Eden beamed at me, his eyebrows raised and his mouth open in a gesture of excited anticipation.

We stared at each other in an uncomfortable silence for a moment, then I spoke. "You must be joking. Me?" I laughed, waves of shock and embarrassment coursing through my body. "I may be a person others respect but in no way am I qualified to govern all 10 Regions."

"But you are!" Eden said as he drew up from his couch and knelt beside me, taking my hand gently in his. "Imagine a world unified, not just by currency but in spirit as well, one identity, one union. The people trust you, they listen to you, and you have demonstrated that you have only good intentions." Eden's words danced in my head and tasted like honey.

I answered, "Well, what you say is true, but it is not right for me to judge others, and that is what a king must do. Only Aigonz can judge positive from negative."

Eden moved his face inches from my own, staring deep into my eyes, his breath hot on my lips. "Of all the people in our world, you are the one closest to Aigonz, closest to knowing good from evil," he cooed, drawing so close I could feel the electricity from his smooth cheek buzzing on mine. "The people believe this and it's the reason they trust you. Search yourself. You know it is right for this to happen; providence favors our undertakings."

Eden rose from my side and glided back to his couch, resting comfortably again beneath the leaves. Despite my initial protest I knew he was right. In fact I had often thought that with my connection to Aigonz and the people's overwhelming love for me a change for the better was possible. If I were King I would make a change for good, I thought, for the good of all people. I decided to hear him out.

He continued, "I can see you agree with me. Tell me you do," he said playfully, once more stroking the leaves of the overhanging Dheal tree.

A smile broke over my demure expression and I bowed my head in humility. "Yes, Eden, I believe you are right. I could rule. I could create change and right the wrongs of our world."

"What is the cause of your hesitation?" he asked.

"I hesitate because it is troublesome for me to think that I would be deciding good and evil for so many. What if I made a poor decision? Or more so, what if I am wrong in judging and punishing those who commit offenses? It is an awful thing to punish one undeservedly."

Eden smiled, "And what makes you think it is wrong for one person to judge another? If the judge has only good intentions and clarity of mind, she is quite qualified to distribute punishment."

"Aigonz is the only true judge," I replied confidently. "All other judgment is inferior. There is an ultimate good and an ultimate evil and only Aigonz understands fully the degrees to which these things affect people and our world."

"I agree with you that Aigonz creates law as it applies to society, but there is a higher law, the law of science," said Eden whimsically, sensing he was inciting my ire. "I know it to be true that there is a right for one person that may not be a right for another."

I shook my head in disapproval. "No. I know that is not the case. Evil is evil all the time and good can never be anything other than good. It is the way of things. Why else would we have laws that make certain activities wrong for everyone? Further, you have asked me to be the very person to create laws where wrong and right are rigidly defined. If your claim is true that good and evil are subjective, how can your request be sincere? You are asking me to do the very thing you argue against; in my understanding, good and evil are apparent and universal." I could feel my face flush with heat, upset that a man of such intelligence refused to hear the merit in my words.

Eden smiled at me, "See, I have spoken my true thoughts and they have cost me a high price. I have angered you." I waved my hand in a gesture of submission and urged him to continue.

"It is true that, for the sake of social order, there must be well-defined laws to ensure society continues to function, but in the grand scheme of things, when we separate social law from universal truth, we find strictly defined morality as merely a device to secure order. Look to science, my friend, and you will find I am correct."

"Eden, I don't understand how science provides morality. But beside that, are you suggesting Aigonz is inferior to science? That the Supreme Being is not the ultimate judge?" I was beginning to worry about my friend. He seemed so wonderful at first, but now was questioning everything I knew to be true.

Eden never looked away, never broke his smile, but answered calmly and lucidly, his fingers joined together at the tips and resting on his chest. "I understand your concern over my comments and I truly meant no harm by saying them.

But I have discovered that there is an entirely different world boiling beneath the surface of our own, a world that reveals truth to whomever asks the right questions and has the courage to recognize it. Aigonz may exist to create social order, but fundamental Reality is to be found right here, on the planet we inhabit, in the things we can see and touch. Science tells us this is so."

"Are you saying that Aigonz doesn't even exist, that It is a product of our imagination designed solely to structure society?" The thought of this was alarming to me and I was beginning to see my new friend as not so friendly after all.

Once again, Eden answered as though he could read my thoughts. "Do not upset yourself. My personal views are unimportant next to the reality of corruption in our Regions. Let's not burden ourselves with technicalities. No amount of disagreement will help our neighbors in distress."

But his attempt to comfort me did not work. I answered passionately, "Your personal views do matter to me because you are in essence asking me to represent you before the world, to help you realize your plan for everyone. If your plan is not the right one I will not be coerced into supporting false doctrine."

Eden's eyes grew soft, a spring of compassion bubbling to the surface of his facade. "But we have just been introduced and already we argue. Perhaps we need more time to become acquainted."

"Perhaps you are correct," I sighed. Suddenly, an idea came to me. I broke my look of concern and smiled at him. "But two minds such as ours will not lightly dismiss so heady a topic as this. It is too important. So it seems only appropriate that we have this discussion not behind closed doors but in the most public of forums. We should debate," I said.

Eden shifted on his couch, turning his shoulder to me and facing back toward the Governor's palace. "A debate?

Before the Governors and Nobles?"

"That is the tradition," I answered. In my world, public figures who found themselves in disagreement would often times present their cases in a forum, presided over by the Governors. These debates would often be broadcast to all Regions, letting the people observe for themselves how Nobles settled disputes. The worst part, though, was that a debate would sometimes end in shame for the loser. In the past, Nobles had been publicly disgraced by losing a debate, humiliated before the entire world. But my convictions were so strong I would risk this in order to establish the truth. "We will let the Governors decide."

"Very well," Eden sighed, throwing his head back and staring into the sky. "If you insist, we will debate," he groaned. "But if I am declared the winner, you must agree to hear my plan for the world with you as King."

"And if I win?" I countered.

"If you win the debate I will alter the way I view Reality. I will take seriously the voice of Aigonz and rely less on science to guide me." I could tell Eden was just saying this to appease me. Still, as he spoke I felt my excitement for him returning and my heated objections yielding to heated flesh.

"This sounds agreeable," I said, smiling softly, touching my cheek to my shoulder as he rose from his couch. I felt more at ease as Eden again came to my side, this time sitting next to me and pulling me close to him. His perfumes were intoxicating and filled my nose, swirled in my mouth. I felt more attracted to him than before, and I sensed my body relaxing and yielding to his embrace. I couldn't stop myself nor did I try.

Eden was speaking softly into my ear, his voice tickling, his breath like sweet grass. "Let's forget all of this for now and just enjoy one another. I would like you to trust me. Do you trust me?"

48

I looked at him, "I want to trust you," I breathed.

"Then let yourself," he whispered, his lips grazing my neck. "I want to know everything about you. Let me know you." His voice was intoxicating, his touch electrifying, and we remained in the quiet of the Governor's garden exploring each other, body and soul.

Segment 4

Debate

4

"Tonight is a special evening for all of us here: those of Noble birth and Governors alike," proclaimed Governor Hiru, ruling power of the Nyanga Region. Her voice resonated through the vast space of the Great Hall. At Hiru's announcement a great roar rose from the crowd, all anticipating the exhibition that was about to begin. I was seated comfortably on the floor of the hall, with Eden sitting on the floor to my left. Nobles from every Region spiraled around us, seated in rows that circled high up into the building. The Great Hall was a familiar meeting place for the Nobles of my world, used to accommodate anything from an athletic event to a public forum of any kind; in this case, a debate[1].

The Great Hall was extremely large, so big, in fact, that I recall its ceiling being almost invisible to a person looking up from the floor. Warm yellow light poured from the higher levels, illuminating the wooden floor polished to an iridescent gold-cloud color. Surrounding the floor was a soft black cloth which covered much of the massive Hall, cloth so thick the Nobles' feet sunk when they walked on it.

Eden and I sat cross-legged on the very center of the floor, the din of clambering Nobles around us, each arguing with the other about the night's possible topics. Many Nobles held cups filled with Eden's refreshment-drink, a recipe that had become extremely popular among the aristocrats in the months since Eden and I were first introduced. I waited with anxious anticipation for the exhibition to begin, and wondered if Eden felt the same. Every time I looked over at him, though, he appeared absolutely unaffected by the grandeur of the event.

After what felt like an eternity, Hiru called for quiet and the crowd reluctantly obliged, settling into their seats and ordering their new favorite drink be replenished. "We have before us a debate, a challenge set forth by the Noble to my right, one who I am sure does not require the benefit of an introduction." Governor Hiru smiled and turned in my direction. As the Governor welcomed me, the Nobles sounded their approval and I rose from the floor, signaling to them my thanks for their warm greeting. After some time the crowd subsided and the Governor turned away to continue her announcements.

"The man to my left has been challenged. As most of you are aware, he has come to prominence through his theory of limitless energy. He has been honored as one of the greatest scientific mind our world has ever known and is currently working with the Governors to develop his energy plan for us all. Please do not hesitate to welcome Edensaw Megedagik Tasapainottaa." A greeting equal to the one given me thundered from the audience. Eden stood and lifted his arms in a gesture of gratitude, his colorful robes glowing even brighter in the light of the stage. The 9 remaining Governors sat along the very front of the crowd and rose to their feet in respect for Eden. He has made some great progress in winning over the Regional powers, I thought, as the Governors joined in sounding their approval.

Governor Hiru continued as the noise for Eden faded. "As you know, the winner of this debate is to be determined by the board of Governors. The terms of the debate have been agreed upon by both parties and it is to be considered a friendly contest, with the winner claiming no rights beyond the authority of this forum." Eden and I had grown quite close in the months before the debate and decided there would be no formal penalty for the loser; this debate was simply an exhibition. Still, there was much riding on the outcome. The People of the world respected and loved me as one of their own, but debate results were always made public and a loss could damage my standing among them. But I had issued the challenge, perhaps in haste, and now had to make good on it.

Hiru turned to me, "You have issued the challenge and therefore must begin." A hush stole over the audience as Eden and I both rose. Eden walked to the side of the stage and left me alone in the center of the glowing floor. I began.

"I would like to introduce this debate by quoting a famous artisan of our time. It has been said that even the greatest knowledge should be questioned, even the greatest words be reformed, and even the greatest person be held accountable." A ripple of murmurs swept across the attendees, as all recognized the reference. I turned to Eden. "A few short months ago my friend and I, being barely acquainted, met to discuss affairs of the world. During this discussion we drifted to matters of great importance, not only to the world but to our perception of Reality[2] as we know it.

"Throughout time, people have pursued a way to view the world, seeking a sense of what is real, a branch to grasp as we fight our way through the mire of ignorance. As you all know I have been privileged to face death, to succumb to it, and have returned to tell of what I learned. Upon returning to this world, I was struck with the unshakable conviction that there is more to Reality than comes to the senses[3]. I then began my tours and over time have been embraced as a prophet by the People and Nobles alike.

"You have all read my words and listened to my speeches and decided that I am one to be trusted, a person who tells the truth no matter what the result. But as I accept, I am not above question. So it is time here and now to defend questions regarding my views, to restate previous words, and to hold myself accountable before you, Governors, Nobles, and opponent. This is why I am here today, and I will respect your decision as we settle this friendly dispute. Thank you and I invite my friend Edensaw to deliver his opening comments." I stepped back from the center and looked at Eden. He was the same as ever, calm and confident. I remember thinking that he looked especially wonderful in the glow of the Great Hall, and I felt a strong respect for him as he turned and faced the audience.

Eden's voice rang full and clear as he began, "My friends I am over-grateful for this opportunity to have you adjudicate today. My opponent is indeed formidable and my views are admittedly unpopular. But I hold them to be true just the same. From an early age I too was convinced that the world extends beyond what our eyes show us. Then I was introduced to Science[4] and from there began to realize there is more to Reality than we knew—it merely had to be discovered.

"So I probed, dug, and sifted through all we thought to be true and have arrived at a version of Reality I know is superior to the old way, which relies on invisible law-makers and primitive superstition to derive truth. It is from this Reality that I have discovered a way to harness limitless energy. It is from this Reality that I have rendered irrelevant the need for Aigonz[5], whether belief in It be truth or falsehood, as I will articulate today. Governors, I will respect your decision as we settle this friendly dispute." Eden turned to me and said the words all must say in order to formally begin a debate, "The burden is upon you. Please begin."

A great excitement burst from the crowd, acknowledging we were about to start. I waited for the noise to settle and I began. "It was some months ago when Edensaw and I were first introduced. During this meeting we learned much about one another. We realized we share many beliefs in common, but we also discovered we have many differing points of view. One of the most alarming was my opponent's assertion that Aigonz is not the foundation of everything we know to be true. Edensaw has claimed that his belief in Science explains every aspect of our existence and Aigonz is irrelevant except as a superstitious belief to keep social order. As I have informed the world, there is a Reality that cannot be touched or seen but is certainly present in everything. I know you have all heard this before, but I must reiterate for the sake of the debate." Laughter vibrated from the crowd affirming they had indeed heard my theory before, as had the majority of people on earth.

"Under the surface[6] of things, behind the face of every person, between the air we breath and the ground we walk on, is Reality, held together, made whole, completed in Aigonz. That which guides every action, judges every wrong deed, helps the good-hearted is Aigonz. Where is Aigonz? It is a part of you, in everything, yet nowhere to be seen. What is Aigonz? A being greater than you or I that feels as we do, loves as we do, and wants only the best for us. How do we know Aigonz is real? There is an organ[7] within you, your soul, that cannot be removed if it is sick and cannot be seen if you are opened up. Aigonz is there and you can feel It living within you.

"What can we say about Aigonz? We can say Aigonz knows the world we live in because It is the essential ingredient in making the world livable. We can say Aigonz transcends time and space yet is as present as you or me, present even in this room today. We can say Aigonz is the judge of good and evil, for certainly good and evil exist and have been presented to us by It, by virtue of Its unifying presence in everything. When did Aigonz come into being? From the beginning of this world we have known Aigonz.

"But Aigonz was not created by us, or as my friend and opponent may suggest, born of imagination. Aigonz was already there to be discovered. Before my death-experience I was informed of Aigonz but gave It no mind, for I felt It had no bearing on my life. But when my eyes were opened I could see Aigonz in everything. With that deep sight came the knowledge that Aigonz has existed long before my time and will endure long after." The audience murmured their agreement and shifted in their seats as I paused for a moment. I looked at Eden and saw he was staring at me intently, arms folded on his chest, seemingly enraptured by my speech.

I continued, "With these things understood as a fact of Reality, who among us will say Aigonz is not the supreme judge to which all moral opinions must defer? Who will say that Aigonz is a creation of our minds merely to keep society in order? My opponent says this. He says Science can replace Aigonz with proof that can be seen and observed. He says Science answers every question the existence of Aigonz once did. But such statements ignore the fundamental truth that has been revealed to me, a truth that goes beyond my agendas and my intentions. This is a truth I have been commissioned to tell to the world, a truth that must be recognized if the world is to right itself and people are to live a good life. I know these things to be truth, I don't simply believe them. I was removed from my body and instructed in truth and I say Aigonz is real and residing among us!" I threw my arms up in a triumphant gesture of victory, my voice resounding through the Hall. The audience pounded their feet into the ground in a show of approval, and the sound of their stomping rolled around the Great Hall in fantastic waves of power. After many moments[8] of this the applause subsided and Eden strode forward to address the people in attendance, joining me in the center of the floor.

I turned to watch as Eden faced the panel of Governors and began. "I know, my friends, that the person of Aigonz is important to our world. It is a unifier[9], this much I admit, and It has existed perhaps as long as we have, at least here on earth. Aigonz is a part of our lives, and should continue to be as It is responsible for keeping many on a path toward good deeds. Aigonz brings together people of all Regions and is a figure to which we can appeal in times of distress or use as an explanation when things become confusing. I am not suggesting that we change the way we live, for it has worked well until now, but I do believe there is an alternative when considering the nature of Reality, the truth about the way things work.

"Science has shown me a different explanation for the force[10] that binds things together. You may ask, what is it that keeps my feet on the ground or makes a rock hard? Some say Aigonz does this, but I say Science has an answer. You see my friends, there are laws that all objects must obey. These are not laws created by a superhuman presence but by the very objects themselves. For example, our feet remain on the ground not because Aigonz wills it but because our feet can do nothing other than stay on the ground. The earth moves and is shaped in such a way that things stick to it, like this building, or stones in the field, or our very feet. According to Science, Aigonz did not do this; one need look no farther than the earth itself for the answer.

"But what is it that keeps a rock in the shape of a rock, that it doesn't turn to sand? Surely this is the work of Aigonz, binding things together to create the world we experience. It is my opinion that this step is not necessary, for again Science provides a different point of view. You see, all things, a rock or a tree or your clothes or your bodies, are made up of much smaller pieces of material, pieces that cannot be seen as individual parts. For example, when we look at a building we see a single structure, but this structure is made of many different parts that all work together to create one unified object. The same is true with a rock. Science tells us a rock is composed of many different parts all working together to create one unified object. These parts have a unique way of attracting each other and do so using the same laws that keep our feet on the ground—they could not behave in any other way. Now, we may break a rock, crush it into sand, but the parts remain unchanged. Imagine that we destroy a building. We are able to see many materials used to construct the building when it is destroyed, but the materials have not changed, they have simply been disrupted, separated from each other, and they no longer represent a building. The building has a new shape—that of a destroyed building. When a rock is ground into sand the rock has taken on a new shape—that of a ground up rock."

Eden paused for a moment and looked around. I was listening intently to his speech so I might argue more effectively, but I was also taking in the demeanor of the Governors and the audience in general. Some people clapped their hands in protest to what Eden was saying, but most seemed to be listening with rapt attention. Eden had a way of presenting things so people could not possibly think he was wrong, and he had such a charming manner and trusting smile that he could sell units to a Collector. But I knew in my heart he was wrong. Maybe Science could explain some things that Aigonz did not but I knew my experience of death and rebirth and I knew the knowledge I gained through this experience was true.

Eden continued, "My friend argues Aigonz has existed as long as there have been people on earth, and to this claim I must acknowledge agreement. In some form or another, Aigonz has been a part of the history of this world, perhaps called by different names at different times, perhaps adorned with this attribute or that. But this does not prove Science wrong. This simply means that as long as there have been humans they have imagined an Aigonz to explain things that could not otherwise be explained. Nobles, the time to imagine a superhuman[11] existence is past and a new era of knowledge is upon us. Science has revealed the truth to us, truth that explains the most detailed workings of the world without the aid of Aigonz. Aigonz is not dead, though. As long as It remains in the imagination It is as real as It ever was. But for those of you who wish to experience the world to its fullest, another reality is yours for the taking."

I was furious with Eden for making such wild claims, claims that completely flew in the face of what I knew to be true. I responded by facing the audience once more and speaking, "Edensaw certainly has a valid claim to the role of Science in the scope of Reality, but he is missing a fundamental truth. Aigonz is real, a force that permeates and unifies. Aigonz is actuality. Science may inform us in matters of macro-reality, but it is the Reality that exists behind the macro that Aigonz informs. Surely I can say any number of things about a rock and never mention the name Aigonz, but in order to truly understand a rock, Aigonz must be present."

Eden answered, "But my friends, this is simply not the case. My opponent is correct in claiming Aigonz need not be mentioned when speaking of Reality, and this is where the argument should end. Those who disapprove of Science say 'show me proof that your claim is true,' and Science happily obliges. Those who disapprove of Science say 'Aigonz is real because we know It is,' and Science shows them Aigonz is not necessary. My challenge to all who believe Aigonz exists is, show me proof of Its existence, proof I can see or touch or otherwise experience, and I will believe. But please be assured this will not happen. It does not exist anywhere but in the imagination."

"But there is proof," I said. "Search your soul and there you will find Aigonz. Be honest about your feelings and there you will find Aigonz. Look to the good that exists in the world and there you will find Aigonz." My voice rose in passion, "There is not one among us who can deny I speak the truth." Applause thundered from the audience and I nodded to my friend across the stage.

Eden's eyes sparkled as he stared into mine, waiting for the noise to die. Then he spoke, "I am one who denies this. I have searched my soul and found no space for Aigonz. My feelings are as they appear to me, bent toward Scientific explanation. And as far as good in the world, my friends, I find not enough to go around. If Aigonz exists It would do well to provide more good for more people because, in the world I live, people suffer."

"People suffer as a result of their own choices, not by the will of Aigonz," I said.

"So the cripple chose to be born as such, correct?"

I faltered, "Well, Aigonz has many unusual and secret reasons for allowing suffering."

"And what of the mother who has lost three children to disease? Was that her choice to suffer so?"

"The will of Aigonz is not always known. We must believe and trust It has our best interests at heart." My skin began to flush as I felt myself faltering under the weight of Eden's arguments. I'd heard these questions before and responded in the same way but this time it didn't seem like it was enough.

He answered, "Science does not rely on such mysteries. Science tells us the cripple is born because of problems in the womb. Science also tells us that disease affects certain functions of the body and so can explain to the grieving mother why her children succumbed. More so, Science can look at these problems and attempt to develop remedies to prevent the same sufferings in the future. Aigonz does not do this. Aigonz watches while people suffer; Science tries to help." The audience rustled nervously and stared at me, waiting for a response, as Eden beamed.

"Aigonz is a part of our system of good and bad, right and wrong, positive and negative. If for no other end, Aigonz is here to judge the wicked and reward the benevolent." I was nervous at this point. I was losing the debate.

"You are correct. Aigonz is part of our system of good and bad, but only because we have made It so. There is no superhuman judge watching and evaluating the nuance of every human experience. Good and bad are relative notions, different for every person."

I countered, "So it is your claim that good is not so for every person. You are saying that for every person it is not good to obey the law[12]?" This is my chance to revive my argument, I thought.

"There are cases where the law is different than the one we enjoy. Is it not true that laws have changed over time? Recall a time when it was not permitted to leave one's home Region under penalty of punishment. Now travel between Regions is not only lawful, it is encouraged. Has Aigonz changed the ultimate good regarding this law? Did Aigonz say, 'I have changed my mind, what was once evil is now good?' Certainly you must admit this is the case if Aigonz represents Reality."

"But this is an example of a law of the People, not a universal law set forth by Aigonz." I was scrambling to recover at this point, seeing he had the best of me. "The good and evil proclaimed by Aigonz transcends transient human law."

"Tell us, then, what is an example of an evil deed that Aigonz has declared ultimately evil for all, no matter the circumstance?"

"The evil of murder," I said grimly. "The ending of an innocent life is an evil action from which none can escape."

Eden replied, "But we see people die every day in the center of every city in every Region. Those poor wretches stuffed in cages swinging above our heads are as good as dead, yet not all are guilty."

"If they are not guilty they would not be there," I

answered.

"But these people are only guilty by the transient human law, to use your words, not the law of Aigonz. By our law, a starving, unitless woman who has stolen bread to feed herself and her children will be sentenced to swing if she is caught. Would Aigonz' law declare her innocent or guilty?"

"I must say she is innocent in the eyes of Aigonz. For although she violated a human law, I feel it is the right of every person to survive and provide for the survival of her children," I said.

"I agree this may not be an evil deed for her even though it violates our law. But if she dies in her cage, as she well might, are we not then murderers? We have killed an innocent person, thus violating what you claim to be a universal, superhuman law. So you admit that in this circumstance what is evil for one person is not so for another?"

I stammered, "I admit nothing to that effect. You have used trickery to distort the debate and bend the conversation to your advantage." Even as I said those words I knew I was defeated. But his slippery words were not enough to shake my faith and I was becoming confused, not sure how to salvage my already sinking argument.

Eden continued, addressing the stunned audience, "This is not trickery but simply sound reason[13]. Science tells us that there can be no absolutes, that everything is changing all the time. Science measures these changes and makes predictions for the future based on current conditions and past experience. Aigonz tells us there are rigid absolutes that cannot be altered despite the situation. This is an inaccurate representation of Reality. Thus, the need for Aigonz is no more. Let us look to Science to help make our lives better." Shouts of approval broke out from the audience, but this time in favor of Eden's words and not mine. I have lost, I thought.

But my faith[14] held strong. I issued my final words, "I

have communed with Aigonz, have seen It and felt It and been enveloped in It for years now. I know Aigonz exists and will take that knowledge to my tomb," I said. "Science can never replace what Aigonz has given me—a second life. Aigonz brought me back from the dead. Science cannot. With these words I am finished."

Eden turned to me and said, "My friend, claiming something is so does not make it fact. Aigonz exists in the imagination and nowhere else. If we remove Aigonz from our imagination our world will continue as it always has, unaffected by a deity. Science has replaced Aigonz as the best way to explain the world. With these words I am finished."

The crowd jumped to their feet. The boom of shouting voices resounding throughout the Great Hall signaling the end of the debate. I hung my head as the Governors deliberated among themselves, deciding which of us was to be declared the winner. Eden and I sat back in the center of the shimmering floor. I stared at the ground, Eden's words swirling in my head. 'Could I be mistaken?' I asked myself. Eden made so much sense, yet I could not bring myself to believe him. I glanced up at him and noticed he was sitting comfortably, glowing, I thought, from his obvious victory. He was looking around the Hall, smiling at the Nobles who were gesturing their respect for him from across the room. I looked back down and waited for the result.

Governor Hiru broke from the deliberation and strode to the center of the stage. "We have deliberated and have come to a decision." She walked over to me, leaned down and kissed me on the cheek. "You've won," she whispered, her hands gently caressing my shoulders. "Well done, my old friend."

Segment 5

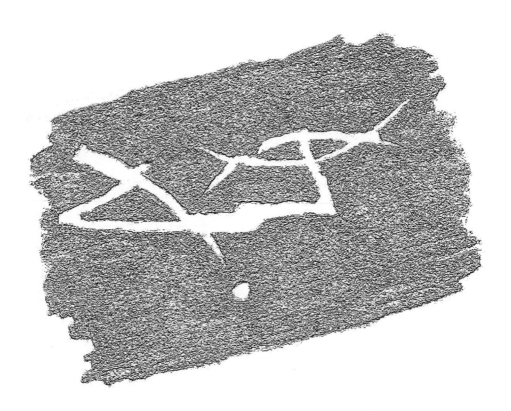

Amaia

5

Why did my beliefs crumble so easily? No matter how hard I thought about it I couldn't figure out what happened. As a traveling prophet I'd been challenged many times in the past, and every time someone questioned me I would always have the right answer, or at least the answer that made them stop asking questions. But not this time.

In the days after the debate I became upset, confused, and started questioning and arguing with myself. I found myself tirelessly defending Aigonz, but no matter how good my argument seemed, Eden's voice would creep in and remind me of some error in my thinking, some scenario where Aigonz could not be the correct answer. I was faced with the possibility that Eden had discovered an entirely new way of looking at things. Sure, there'd been people of Science before Eden but never had one urged so strongly to abandon Aigonz.

I was avoiding him in the days after the debate, mostly from guilt that I was declared the winner and embarrassment from knowing I was defeated. Of course, it wasn't more than a few days before Eden and I reconnected[1]. Despite what happened, I was still very fond of him and thought of him constantly while we were apart.

Immediately after our debate, Eden embarked on his own tour of the Regions, bringing with him his limitless energy design in an attempt to convince the Governors to abandon their previous source of power in favor of his. He was beginning to develop quite a reputation himself, heralded as the greatest Scientific mind of our age, and this distinction only increased his popularity as he traveled among the lawmakers. He was known to hold long, private meetings with the Governors; sometimes two or three Governors at a time would speak with Eden behind sealed doors. I never asked him what went on at these meetings, but now, thinking back, I'm pretty sure I know what they were about.

It was during his tour that I received a message from Eden requesting my presence. I still felt apprehensive about seeing him again but knew it would happen sooner or later. But I also missed his companionship, so I didn't hesitate to meet him at his home in Kurrurbun, a distant Region, bordering the Forgotten Land at its extremity.

I departed Nyanga for Kurrurbun, which had a great city of the same name. It was quite a distance for a single day's journey, but soon enough the buildings rose to greet me from among the dunes, a sprawling desert-city, its infrastructure connected by windswept roads so covered in sand they were at times almost invisible. My transport[2] easily maneuvered through the winding metropolis, disembarking finally at Eden's threshold[3].

Eden's home was modest by our standards, with few servants and space enough for complete privacy. He'd become a hero in his city, but I wouldn't have known it by his possessions, which were scant. The most prized was his laboratory, which sat at the back of his home and dwarfed the living areas. Aside from that, though, the home was sparsely furnished, barely enough furniture to entertain even a few people. A table here, a chair there, hardly lavish by any measure. But Eden lived for one thing, Science, and had little time for anything else. Or course, when I visited, his attention was entirely mine. I was taking in the bare interior of his receiving room when Eden entered, arms extended, a look of warm pleasure on his face.

"I see you are enjoying the treasures of the Great Palace at Kurrurbun[4]," laughed Eden as he walked toward me, his feet clicking on the shining wood floor, resonating through the very large and very empty room.

"Their beauty is eclipsed only by the one they call

Lord," I answered playfully, turning to meet him. We were instantly in each other's arms. "It is wonderful to see you, my friend," Eden breathed as we clutched each other in a welcome embrace. "I trust recent events have not soured me in your eyes?"

"Of course not, dearest companion," I sighed. "My only regret is that it has been so long since we last touched. My hands beg for you."

"And mine for you, dearest companion." He led me into a side room and closed it off to others. After some time spent enjoying much deeper greetings, we found ourselves prepared for conversation. We lounged on a couch, my slight frame stretched over him, my head resting comfortably on his smooth brown chest. After a wonderful silence, I began with a question that had been consuming me for some time.

"Eden, why was I declared the winner of our debate?" I asked.

He laughed softly and said, "Because yours was the most convincing argument."

"But we both know that is not true," I said.

"It is true, friend," he said, rubbing my shoulder with his rough, powerful hand. "You received the kiss and therefore you are the winner. I hold no grudge or animosity because of it. I only wish it was I who had the pleasure of kissing you."

"No, of course you don't harbor resentment. You are not that type of person, nor did I expect you to be. But nevertheless, it is so very curious to me that you did not prevail. Your arguments were far superior to mine. There was a point when I felt I couldn't even form a sentence, so lost was I in my own rhetoric." I was becoming a bit upset remembering the event and Eden stroked my hair in a gesture of comfort.

"Look, it was a friendly debate with no lasting consequences. Were those not the terms we agreed upon?"

His voice was like water for my parched ears.

"Yes," I said, "those were the terms of our arrangement. But Eden, I have been so confused lately. I feel like I don't know what to believe anymore." I pulled myself up so I could look him directly in the eye, our noses almost touching. My long hair draped like curtains beside me, falling on Eden's face and the cushions beneath him. "All of what you said made sense to me and I have spent the past few weeks turning my mind inside out trying to come to some agreement between what I know and what you say. It has been so difficult and troublesome." I buried my head in his chest and began to cry, hot tears of disconnection[5] poured from my bursting eyes. But Eden was firm as a glacier, and my tears dripped from him like water from ice during the warm months.

Eden kissed my head, "It is best, my dearest friend, if we do not speak of this for now. Let us instead use our time together not for tears but for enjoyment."

I sniffed and drew up from him, wiping the liquid from his glistening body. "You are right," I sniffed, "we have much to discuss." I looked at him and smiled. We stood and regained our composure, donning clothing and situating ourselves to face one another so we might continue our conversation.

"You know, Eden," I said, "in all the time I've known you you've never actually told me how your energy machine works. Won't you tell me now?"

Eden seemed elated with enthusiasm at my question. He pulled his flask from inside his robe and, after a long swallow, wiped his mouth and eagerly began explaining. "Well, I call the machine Amaia[6], and it is the safest form of energy possible. Currently we use different methods to create power to use in our daily lives. We have discovered how to harness the energy of the sun, but as you know it yields little and is almost impossible to transfer over any significant distance. We also create power from water, but of course, virtually all water is frozen for the majority of the year and cannot be used in that state. There are a few other methods but the result is the same for all of them—little energy yield and no longevity.

"Now this is not a problem for the Governors because each has her own energy supply in her palace and surrounding land and so does not care for the plight of the common person. Nobles as well can all afford the best technologies available yet share none of this with the People. Not only is it unfair, the technology they use is dated and inefficient.

"But with Amaia, all people can have all the power they need, distributed at no cost and with no limits. The power of the sun, the power of the water: these are costly, limited sources. Amaia will produce lossless, infinite energy for us to use. Imagine a world where machines could do our work for us, leaving us time to relax and truly live our lives. We have the machines but they're impractical because they require more power than we can provide. Imagine a world where buildings can be built not in months or years but in weeks, days, all because we have the power to do so."

Eden paused and leaned back on his couch, studying my face for signs of approval. It's true that, while my world had in fact created machines to make our lives more comfortable, we could not provide the amount of power needed for these machines to be available to everyone, regardless of social rank. It had also become more difficult to provide energy to the machines that were available to the People, like the Beltway, and other machines designed to preserve life. Taking these things into consideration I could think of nothing negative about what he was saying.

"That all sounds very good to me, Eden. This is certainly a positive thing you are doing, trying to help people by improving their lives. It's true that many social problems could be remedied if only we had more energy to give."

"Yes, it is true," he said. "This is the greatest step our world can take."

"But how does Amaia produce its power?" I wondered.

Eden laughed, "Well, it's all very technical but I can give you the basics."

"I would like that very much," I said.

"Do you remember during our debate when I spoke of things being composed of smaller materials, I gave the example of a building, or better yet, a rock?"

"How can I forget," I laughed.

"Well, this is the reality of the physical world. Matter[7] is made up of tiny pieces that all come together to form what we see and touch. Now, it is true that we may tear down a building or grind a rock into sand and see all the materials they were made from. In the case of the rock, when we grind it into sand we will see individual pieces, very tiny pieces in fact, that once went into creating that rock. When we have ground the rock so far down that all that is left are these particles we are inclined to say, 'That's as far as we can go with this. These pieces cannot be ground any smaller.' But this is not true. Science has discovered a way to cut very small pieces of matter in half. We began doing so and discovered a whole world of building materials we never thought were there, so small that your eye or my eye could not see them without the aid of a machine."

"But what good is this?" I wondered aloud.

"At first it wasn't doing us any good; we were left with very small pieces of matter and that was all. Other scientists stopped cutting matter altogether, saying it was useless to do so. But I thought differently. The further I went the more I began to understand there was more beneath the surface than simply more of the same stuff. I soon discovered that if I cut the very smallest pieces of matter, a great deal of energy was released. It was not long before I was able to contain and harness this energy on a small scale. I do not need to collect the sun's heat, I do not need to rely on the motion of the water. All I need is the equipment and the resources and I can produce limitless, lossless power." Eden stood from his couch triumphantly, putting his arms behind his head and looking down at my reclining figure.

I was very happy for Eden and for the world. Finally, I understood. This was what had all the Nobles talking, this was what he and the Governors were discussing. "Eden, I don't understand why you are encountering any opposition to this. The Governors would be fools not to take advantage of your wonderful discovery. Is Amaia safe?"

"Amaia is completely safe," he said without hesitation. "There is no possibility of anything going wrong using my matter-splitting technology. In fact, the very laws of Science tells us that it is impossible for the energy released to have any negative effect on humans."

"So all we do is throw something in and Amaia does the cutting?"

"Well, therein lies the problem. I wish it were as simple as using any piece of matter, but unfortunately it is not. Amaia requires a certain type of rock, more specifically, a deposit of minerals, which scientists call a crystal. There is one very special crystal that contains within it the particles Amaia needs to produce energy."

"What is this crystal called?" I asked.

"It is called Tree-stone[8], named so because, when split, the pieces break into a pattern resembling tree leaves."

"And where does Tree-stone come from?"

"Tree-stone is difficult to find. There is some in the eastern Regions, but little is known about where to find the quantities I need to power all 10 Regions. Some have said there are large deposits in the Forgotten Land." When he said this he paused for just a moment, his voice trailing off. For the first time since we met I noticed a look of sadness, maybe even anger in Eden's eyes. His mention of the Forgotten Land caused this look. Curious, I thought.

"Are you well?" I asked, concerned for his well being.

Eden shook his head, as if breaking free from some shackles keeping his mind prisoner. He smiled at me, "Yes, I am well," he sighed. "I am simply saddened by the thought of this wonderful progress being halted by greedy Governors."

"You have explained that this technology is safe for all. Is it difficult to construct Amaia?"

"It is not difficult to construct but it will require many units. However, the amount needed is more than available in every Region, though the Governors know it will come from their purses."

I became very excited, "But I hold more sway with the Governors than anyone. Surely with my endorsement they will agree to make Amaia a reality for all."

"This possibility has already been explored. The Governors respect you but they will not budge. The only way is to force them to build Amaia."

"How do we force them?"

"The only way is to get the People behind Amaia. The People can be used as a bargaining tool to persuade the Governors. They know that between us, we have the ability to move huge amounts of people toward our cause. And the best part of this is, the People will be easy to persuade. The Fear that is being used right now is focused around energy production, the very thing you and I wish to remedy. The People are already demanding what we need from them, so it will be nothing to sell Amaia. Once the People demand it be built, the Governors will concede. It is like we're using their own tactics against them, but this time in the name of good. Right now is the best time to rally the People toward building

Amaia; they must demand it be built."

This is my area of expertise, I thought. My popularity among the People had intensified to the point that I was recognized everywhere, in every corner of every Region, and I was revered as Aigonz' representative on earth. The People were my children and I was their caretaker; all I needed to do was speak and they would do what I said.

Finally, I thought, I can create some good here on earth. "I could convince them, Eden!" I said. "I will tell the People everything you told me and together we will force the greedy Governors to accept your vision for the Regions. The possibilities are endless!" My mind soared with thoughts of the good that would come with Amaia put into place. An end to hunger, an end to conflict, comfort and leisure for all. No longer would we be slaves to the weather. No longer would those with the least units starve for lack of food. We could build huge climate-controlled buildings for growing endless food supplies year round. Once we erase people's needs we could erase suffering. All these things I considered as we sat for a moment in silence.

Eden broke my reverie, "The possibilities are indeed endless, my dearest friend, as is the energy. If you could use your influence to somehow help me create change you would be doing our world a great service."

Shivers ran through my body, "To be honest, after I received the gift of second-life[9], I wondered what my purpose was. What was Aigonz' reason for bringing me back from the dead? I feel now more than ever that I have finally discovered my purpose. I was put on earth to complete this task, to free the People from their bonds, to bring joy and happiness to all. I know this is Aigonz' will; I know this is the right thing to do. This is my duty."

I remember rising from my couch and embracing Eden where he stood. My body pulsed with the knowledge that

I was about to change everything. He held me and spoke reassuringly as we discussed the best way to proceed with our plan.

Segment 6

Yarakai Kartavya

6

I left Kurrurbun filled with a sense of optimism and more enthusiasm than ever about the future. Still, though I discovered my life's purpose, I wrestled with my own beliefs. While I felt more than ever Aigonz was a reality, in some ways I doubted Its existence. But everyone knows Aigonz is real, it's not even a question. No one before ever questioned, 'Is Aigonz real?' It was always accepted that It was. The more popular question in my world was, 'What is Aigonz like?' Why do so many people see It in so many different ways?

There were many during my age who claimed Aigonz was a force so present that It was like a human, with a body like ours and relationships as we might have. Others said Aigonz was completely unknowable, invisible and fleeting, with no involvement in a person's life. But the longer I thought the more I realized there was one view of Aigonz that stood out above the others. It was old in my memory, buried under years of other experiences and presented to me by a very important person in my life, the person responsible for changing everything I knew about Reality. That person was my murderer.

Do not forget, long before I wrote the words you are reading I was dead, at least for a short time. The man who did this to me left an impression I would never forget, and in fact his words were some of the most profound recollections from my previous life. "Aigonz, do your work through me" was burned into my memory. What does this statement mean, I wondered? The man said these words immediately before plunging a needle into my chest, intent on killing me. Does this mean that, in his mind, Aigonz' work included murder?

Murder was strictly forbidden for followers of Aigonz and this fact was as real to me as any belief I held. But I was starting to realize I might have been mistaken in my views of

Aigonz, that there may be more to It than I realized. I decided I must find my murderer and confront him, question him, and attempt to have him explain his knowledge of Aigonz to me.

In my world, this was far from impossible, especially for a Noble of my standing. As you remember, most convicted criminals were kept in cages above the cities, but certain criminals were housed in institutions designed to separate them from others because of their particularly dangerous nature. As a society we realized that the mentally infirm were likely to kill others if committed to the cages, causing such chaos that they had to be quarantined. There were three such institutions available for use by all 10 Regions, and since meticulous records were kept, it would not be difficult to locate my antagonist. After some informal inquiries I discovered his name and where he was housed and made it a point to travel there and speak with him as quickly as possible.

Walking through the corridors of the Quarantine[1] was no easy task; the smell of human excrement, the howls of torment, the crack of the control devices[2] used to persuade its residents back into their enclosures could not be ignored. I noticed some residents were sitting quietly in their enclosures, neither motion nor emotion evident from their rigid, lifeless expressions.

My guide stared at me as we walked toward our destination. "It certainly is an honor to meet you, Prophet," he said. His eyes gleamed like two bright moons and his face beamed with a smile that looked as though it would burst through his skin. "I have seen your face many times and heard you speak as well." His voice gushed with enthusiasm and he grabbed at my garments as he spoke, "Your treatise changed my life. I am a follower of Aigonz now and live to do Its work."

"I am deeply humbled by your praise, faithful follower," I said softly, reverently, a tone I always kept with the People. "You have done well to listen to my words and keep my guidance close to your heart." Even though I meant what I said I was horribly disconnected by the thought of facing my killer. The guide didn't notice my distraction and continued his stream of consciousness. "I must warn you, Prophet, the person you seek is one of the most dangerous and uncontrollable in the Region, possibly in the whole world, so dangerous, in fact, that he is kept pinned to the wall of his enclosure day and night, held back from his destructive tendencies."

"I thank you for your concern," I said and bowed my head in anxious anticipation. But even this advice could not prepare me for what was to come.

The man was standing with his back to the wall of a clean but uninviting room, an enforced window opposite him spraying the afternoon sun unnoticed on the gray floor. The walls were made of a cold metal with many hooks and fasteners spotting the area around where he was lashed. An obviously unused bed sat opposite the man, under the window, covered in a fine mesh screen no doubt electrified to prevent escape.

Escape would not be a possibility for my choice company, though. The man was fixed[3] to the wall with cuffs on both wrists and ankles, splaying him like the limbs of a festival animal atop the feast-fire. His head was covered by a soft mask that opened at the mouth, holding the tongue down and keeping his teeth from touching. This too was attached to the wall as was a belt at his waist, forcing complete immobility. "A fine sight, this one is, agree?" the care-worker said to me as he loosed the man's mouth restraint enough to enable talking.

"I'm sure he's seen better days," I managed. To tell the truth, I hadn't thought much about my attacker's appearance in quite some time; the incident was more like a fleeting dream than an actual event. But now, looking at him, I remembered the horror of that night. His dripping, stringy hair hung lifeless over his face, which was covered by a straggly beard. And those eyes, never blinking, half closed with no sign of life and absolutely no recognition of Reality. I stared at the pathetic figure and wondered what could lead a person to find himself in this state. 'Surely this man has chosen this path for himself,' I thought; 'Aigonz is punishing him for his misdeeds.'

"What is his name?" I asked my guide.

"He calls himself Yarakai Kartavya[4]," the care-worker said. At the mention of his name Yarakai sprang to life, metal fasteners clanking as he struggled in his restraints. I was startled at the sudden commotion and jumped back in fear. His eyes, in the Ground-Finder almost closed and completely lifeless, were wide and alert, blazing with inner-fire[5] as he let loose two long screams from his unchecked mouth and squirmed to get free.

"Calm down, Yarakai, you have a guest," the care-worker said in an uninterested voice, pulling a needle from his belt and administered a sedative. "This will make him calm but he will still be able to talk." The guard made some final checks of Yarakai's restraints and said, "I'll leave you two alone now. Just be careful and don't get too close. This man is very dangerous and can't be trusted." I nodded knowingly and assured him all would be fine as the man exited the room.

So there I was, as before, defenseless and face to face with my killer. Yarakai's struggle calmed as the sedative took effect and as he settled he began to weep softly. I felt so much pity for this wretched man. What must his reality be like? I wondered. I called his name, urging him to look at me. He lifted his eyes from the ground and as he did his expression changed from one of sorrow to one of terror. As I stood face to face with him, I watched his tears stop and a look of deep fear wash over him at the sight of me. His eyes grew glassy and large, his brows furrowed and his lips trembled, foam dripping from the corners of his mouth.

"Please don't kill me," he mumbled. His voice was high like a child's, light and breathy, and trembled pitifully.

"I'm not here to kill you," I answered.

"Yes you are!" Yarakai screamed, his face contorting into a savage snarl. "You want to kill us all!" He thrashed, writhed, twisted his body so much that for a moment I was afraid he would escape his restraints. Realizing it was useless to struggle, he tensed his body and screamed for help, for someone to come save him from the killer in his enclosure. Despite the tension of the situation, I thought it amusing that he was a killer yet he thought he was the one in danger of being killed.

I waited for him to calm down enough to hear me, and when he finally did I spoke reassuringly. "I'm not here to kill anyone, I don't want to kill anyone, I just want to talk to you."

Yarakai stared into my eyes and began a soft laugh that grew in intensity, culminating in a bellow. "Of course you are here to kill us!" he laughed. "It is your duty to do so." He whispered, "That is why I must kill you." I shivered at his sincerity, his words carrying such conviction that I was certain he genuinely believed everything he was saying.

"And why do you think I want to kill everyone?" I asked.

"Because Aigonz told me you do, and It does not lie." Yarakai stared at me in fear, as if expecting me to lash out at him and end his life right there. When I did not react his tone abruptly changed to a mocking taunt. "But you know Aigonz doesn't lie, don't you Prophet," he sneered. "You, the most beloved person on earth, and all because of me, because I couldn't kill you. Now you have returned to take revenge, to kill us all!" he wailed.

I remained calm in an attempt to ease his emotions. After all, I was not there to argue with him but to gain insight. I spoke lightly, "But I love people, I don't want them dead. I would never kill anyone, not even you, Yarakai."

"You will," he snarled. "You will kill all of us, everyone, unless you are stopped. That is my duty, to kill you - yours is to kill me and mine is to kill you." He lifted his eyes to the ceiling and laughed maniacally, shouting out, "How sweet is the dew of fate; drink now, servant, your reward."

Though this man was obviously deranged, I still felt he could be of some use. I waited for him to calm himself again and began gently prodding him for more. "Do you know who I am? You call me Prophet, yet you accuse me of murder."

Yarakai was suddenly still. He turned his eyes and as much of his face as he could toward me and we locked gazes, his voice for the first time clear and steady as he spoke, "I know who you were, who you are now, and what you will become. You are the False Hope[6], one sent to lead humanity into the fire. You are said to be a redeemer, a savior to those who have lost their way. When we first met, you were only the potential for such a person. This is why Aigonz told me to dispose of you, for the good of the people, for the good of the world. But I failed, because here you are, set on clearing for all the way to oblivion."

"But you did not fail," I said, walking back and forth in front of him as I spoke. "I did die. In fact, I was dead for hours. But Aigonz found it good to bring me back to the realm of the living, to help the world realize the error of its ways."

"Don't lie to me!" Yarakai yelled, this time in a harsh gritty tone. "You want me dead! You want us all dead!" Just as quickly as he lashed out his head dropped and he spoke as if in a trance. "And one will come from the Great City of the Horn, one sent to deceive the world, to bring about its end!"

Yarakai was convinced I was planning to murder the people of earth and would not talk about anything else, so I decided to change the conversation slightly to address my original motivation for visiting him, to hear his beliefs about Aigonz.

"So you said Aigonz told you to kill me, right?" I asked.

"It is my duty to kill you. I am...it is an evil that must be done." Yarakai's fingers trembled and twisted, the only free motion he had.

"And how do you communicate with Aigonz?"

He laughed and turned his eyes to the ceiling, "Who doesn't communicate with Aigonz? Only those who have plugged their ears, only those who have cut out their tongue, only those who have plucked out their eyes. But still they might hear Its voice in the quietest parts of their mind, urging action, explaining duty."

I remember thinking how close his assessment of Aigonz was to my own. I also knew Aigonz spoke to me through some other sense, a different mode of perception that was just as real as sight or hearing but was at the same time entirely different. It wasn't as if Aigonz' voice could be heard with my ears, but with an inner ear. It was astounding to me to have this verified by a person shackled to the wall because of his need to murder. "So you believe Aigonz speaks to you directly?"

Yarakai grew quiet again, "I said what I said. If there is one thing that is real in life it is that a person has her own duty to perform. Before your career as a Prophet you were a Collector. Think back on that time now and tell me if it was your duty to increase your unit collection."

I thought for a moment, "No, I must say it was not my duty to be a Collector. I was to become a Prophet, to lead people in the right knowledge that Aigonz has given me."

He became livid. "And what happens when that knowledge is not right? Are you listening? What then? The earth will swallow its parasites, their future imprisoned in time a guarantee!"

I remained calm despite his senseless rantings and answered, "But my knowledge is right. And in a way, you helped me realize this by killing me. Had you not done so I would still be a Collector, oblivious to Aigonz' will, as would the world of followers I have won."

"Aigonz, save us all," the man muttered. "We are all doomed."

I implored, "But don't you see, I want to help people, to save people, to show them a different way of thinking."

"You can help them by breaking your own neck," Yarakai spat.

"So what is Aigonz to you?" I pressed.

He laughed again, his eyes back toward the ceiling. Then, after a few deep breaths, he spoke with the calm and composure of a Noble, his voice completely different from the one I'd just heard, low and smooth, as if he'd become possessed by another person. "Aigonz to me is the voice in my mind, the urge in my limbs, the breath on my lips, the dirt on my feet, the wind through my hair. All of these things tell me you will bring the world down, reduce it to ice, destroying all who dare live during these times."

Again, I was struck by how similar our views were. "What if I told you I agreed with you, that Aigonz to me is all the things you say It is to you?"

Yarakai looked at me and sneered, "Then you would throw yourself out the window and land on your head!" He became irate, "Don't you see, you will destroy everyone! It will be your doing, your words that will send them off the cliff, into the sea!" He shook in his restraints. "I could not save them, Aigonz! I could not do your work! I have failed!

I have failed!" Yarakai began weeping bitterly, his face shimmering with various different fluids. He lashed his body and screamed out, "Here is your devil before me and you hold me powerless! Aigonz, loose my restraints, let me finish what you have started! Hear me, Aigonz! Why do you ask this of me but leave me powerless to obey? Why? Aigonz! Where are you!"

At the sound of such immense torment the Quarantine workers rushed in and administered another sedative, this time leaving Yarakai nearly unconscious. "Our apologies, Prophet, but for your own safety you must leave," one of the workers said to me. "When he gets like this he becomes more dangerous than we are willing to handle and he must be shut down."

"Yes, I understand." I looked at my murderer, hanging limp, restrained and covered in sweat. The workers replaced his mouth-restraint and wiped some of the moisture from his face. I decided it was time to leave and I turned and headed toward the door. But as I did I heard a faint sound from Yarakai. He was calling my name. I rushed over to him and listened close. His words were tangled in the restraints but I could make out the few he murmured, right before his head dropped into troubled sleep.

"Prophet," he said, "Prophet...duty. Your duty must be done. Prophet, your duty must be done. Prophet, your duty... duty...." And he was silent.

Segment 7

Prophet-King

7

This chamber is stifling and the air is thick with my own breath. Sometimes my head swims and I fall backwards onto the floor. But I must keep writing. I must finish. The ground continues to rumble and I hear the sound of water trickling above me, but of course no water can enter here. I suspect you've noticed great similarities between our worlds. The reason for this will be revealed shortly, but for now I must use my time to explain exactly how I became a King[1], the ruler of all the Regions.

During my time as a prophet I was known as many things. "A miracle from Aigonz," "the one who was reborn," "conquerer of death," the People would call me. There were few places within the 10 Regions I could go and not be recognized. My face was recreated high above the city squares, erected by my followers and devotees. I was an advisor of sorts, you see. I became famous because of my resurrection, but I was loved because of the advice and guidance I provided for so many people.

I composed a short treatise from the Healing-Place verses, a sort of list of the things I learned from my experience with death. I wrote about Aigonz and Its role in shaping Reality. I wrote about how to live life and how to conduct oneself, how to behave in a morally upright way, and what the limits of morality were. Millions of copies of this treatise were produced and distributed all over the Regions before I embarked on what became my first grand tour.

In each Region I stopped for a long visit, traveling around the city and meeting with people, discussing their wants and needs and concerns and questions, all the time expounding on the truth I preached[2]. I was heralded as a sort of god[3], I think, even before my first public appearance— that's how much impact my resurrection had. In order to familiarize the People with my theology, I arranged to have my treatise distributed free of charge just prior to my arrival in each Region. This proved beneficial because it introduced to my followers exactly what my knowledge held for them, and they could formulate questions for me to address when I arrived.

The first tour lasted well over a year as I spent much time in each place I visited. I would give talks to the People from the tops of buildings or, in the more rural areas, from large hillsides, and multitudes would flock to see me, to hear what I had to say, and to ask me questions about Reality. There were sometimes so many people that, standing atop my elevated position, it seemed as though they never ended, like the ice-shelves that look boundless as they disappear into the horizon. So appearing before oceans of people became quite normal for me as I slowly made my way through the Regions, and there wasn't a single destination where I was greeted with anything less.

It was during this time that I became acquainted with not only the masses but the Governors as well. Because I was becoming such a phenomenon, the Governors of each Region went out of their way to become my friends, inviting me to their mansions and allowing me unrestricted freedom to travel and do as I please. As a result of these friendships, I was introduced to an entirely new world—the world of high rule.

There were really only a few Nobles who made the laws and the People always seemed to obey them, no matter how unreasonable. I realized this was made possible by persuading the People to hold a certain opinion that would work to the benefit of a Governor. So if a Governor wanted to, say, increase the amount of interest owed on outstanding debts, she would simply create a Fear, inform the People that the only way to alleviate their fear was to surrender more units, then remove the Fear when the People complied. The People would think they righted some imbalance but in reality they were simply slaves to suggestion.

I have mentioned the People suffered under the weight of oppression, of debt, a servant class to the Noble elite. This was true from an outside perspective, but to the People it was the only reality they knew. They would sometimes go hungry, but never often enough to make them question their leaders. They would sometimes be exposed to the weather, but a Noble was always there to restore them to minimal comfort. So the People learned to rely on the ruling class for their most basic needs. Food, physical well-being, shelter, all of these things were ultimately controlled by the Nobles, with the Governors wielding the highest power.

The sad truth was, though, that during my age the People could never change the system that governed their lives without some kind of physical revolt. But the People weren't like that; most abhorred violence. They simply wanted to live their lives, and did so, kept just ignorant enough to have no urge toward violent resistance against the Nobles. The result was that the People simply had no idea what was actually dictating their lives. They were under the illusion that their rulers listened to their voices, but were in reality being told what to say, how to act, and what to think. Even some of the Nobles didn't realize this condition existed; they fulfilled their roles without a second thought about the affect they had on the People.

What the People didn't realize, and what the Governors were acutely aware of, was that they were a real threat to the entire system, mainly because there was so many of them and so few Nobles and Governors. The same way the sands would bury the road to Kurrurbun, so could the People wash over the highest rulers. So when I came along the Governors recognized in me a person the People would listen to, who could persuade the world, if need be, to think a certain way. Not only that, the People would go wherever I went, a sea of potential enemies of the very small ruling class.

Looking back, it was smart of those who made and enforced the rules to recognize I could assemble an army anywhere at any time using nothing other than my presence. So of course the Governors wanted me to be their friend. They saw me as a threat to their power and tried to keep me close to them, which they did. But power was never my motive; I only wanted to do the work I'd been commissioned to do.

It wasn't until after the success of my first tour that I realized just how important my presence was for the People. Some proclaimed I'd changed their lives during one of my rooftop speeches. Others said my treatise answered questions they'd been asking their entire lives. I was pleased to see such positive effects following my efforts, and consequently I spent the next 15 years touring everywhere, meeting with the top law makers in the world and guiding millions of people along what I considered to be their path to freedom[4].

I'd become such a legendary figure that stories about me started appearing, stories I knew weren't true but made me more popular still. There were stories that I possessed super-powers, had the ability to control the elements, and could create living animals from dust. It was reported that I could lift off the ground without the aid of an elevation machine, and there were stories that I could create food for hungry people out of nothing more than scraps of clothing and a few drops of water. Other people swore they saw me command the sun to stop shining during one of my speeches.

I was even credited with bringing the dead back to life. One man went around swearing I brought back his son after an unfortunate illness left the child lifeless in his home. The man claimed he rushed to me to ask for my aid when I was in his Region. He said I listened to his story and followed him back to his house, where I touched the corpse[5] and commanded it to stand. The boy opened his eyes, got up, and walked into the food storage area, complaining he was hungry. Now, none of the stories were true; I do not have any special power nor did I ever, but at the same time I did not discourage people from telling them. What's more, I never denied that any of the stories were true.

But one of the most fantastic stories was the one that claimed I am the child of Aigonz, sent to bring an important message to my age. People started to see me, not as a person, but as an instance of Aigonz, a living deity, not from this world but appearing here for a moment in time to help others know the truth[6]. I must confess, even as I kneel in this tomb, I in some ways believe this particular story about myself.

Living as a revered god definitely had its advantages. I was never in danger, I was never in any need or want, and I had the privilege of involvement with those who made the rules. It was this involvement that really elevated my status to something more than religious leader, it entered me into the world of global rule, of power and control and showed me the faces behind social decision making. And even there I was never treated badly. The Nobles and Governors all embraced me and went out of their way to be my friends. I attended celebrations of the highest order and became a confidant to the most powerful people on earth. So by the time Eden and I met, everyone sought my council and, I admit, not a few social policies were made as a result of my advice.

This is why Eden's proposal that I assume the position of King was not entirely preposterous. It was clear to me that the Regions had been mismanaged. Over the course of my involvement in world governance I witnessed first hand exactly how things were run. I realized that what was told to the People and what was actually taking place were two very different things. All 10 Governors, without exception, were living outside the law. They could do what they wanted when they wanted to do it and suffered no repercussions for illegal behavior. They manipulated the currency system to benefit themselves and their friends exclusively, with no care as to the impact it had on the People. Basically, the rich only became richer and everyone else spent their lives increasing the wealth of those who already had it. Units were spare among the people but there was no end to the amount collected by the Governors.

Shortly before Eden and I first became acquainted, an agreement was reached that permanently joining the currency systems of all 10 Regions, making it easier for units to be collected by any of the Governors from any Region. But the ruling class' liberties went further than this. The Governors also acted as though the laws did not apply to them. I learned of one Governor who killed a family member during a fit of jealousy. It was never a secret that he did this but it was passed off as if nothing happened. That Governor continued to rule his Region, received the same respect as any law-abiding citizen, and lived his life without punishment. Any one else would have been sentenced to swing in the cages, but because he was a Noble and a person who made the laws he did as he pleased, without fear of reproach.

This is why the notion of becoming King became increasingly attractive the more I thought about it. But there was one concern. How could we convince the Governors to allow themselves to be ruled? Surely they would object to this. It would mean limiting their power and asking them to defer to me when they made decisions. I had spent much time with the Governors and I was sure none of them would sacrifice their position to me, even though we were on very friendly terms. Of course, I thought, the People would love to have me as King.

And I really thought I could help them. Many times

the People would come to me and say they were not properly taken care of, that the sick were not helped, that their homes were not kept up but instead were dilapidated and barely habitable. The People complained that while they sometimes went days with only a little food and water the Governors and the Nobles feasted on the finest our world had to offer, never hungry or without necessity, growing fat on the labor of others. They watched in fear as the desperate were ordered to the cages for not paying their taxes, while Nobles payed nothing yet owned everything.

My best response, though, was to assure them that I would do my best to help, that I would speak to the Governors, but I knew in my heart the only way to help the People was to create change. Until the day Eden assured me I would rule as King, change seemed impossible. This, I thought, was the best way, the only way, to help all of those who hurt. I would allow the Governors and the Nobles to keep their lifestyles intact but I would find ways, compromises, that would provide just a little extra comfort for the People.

So I decided I would take Eden up on his offer. He seemed confident that the Governors would agree to my leadership and I decided to leave it entirely in his hands. Because of the recent joining of the Regions there were meetings scheduled to take place, which would bring all the Governors together. Eden was invited to attend as his limitless energy theory was receiving much attention from the newly formed union. I was also invited as I always was, for I represented the voice of the People and had become relied upon by some of the more conscientious Governors for guidance and moral discussion.

Although I was invited Eden and I thought it best that I not attend the talks, but I did leave tour to travel to Nyanga where the talks were being held. Normally the talks centered around Regional affairs, but this time it was different - this time they were discussing the prospect of having me as their

King. Eden spent days in discussion with the Governors as I waited, anxious the entire time. The better part of me did not expect the Governors to accept me as King, but to my surprise they did, unanimously and without objection. I remember Eden bursting into my rooms. "We did it! They have agreed! You are to be King!" he proclaimed, lifting me up and spinning me around.

"Just like that?" I asked, amazed at how quickly such a momentous decision was made. Eden put me down and I hugged him close, looking up into his shining eyes.

"There has to be more to it, Eden," I said, shaking my head. "The Governors never decide anything that quickly. What did you say? What did they say?"

He laughed softly at my ebullience, released me from our embrace and answered, "There was some concern that the People would reject the idea, but we have decided that each Governor will inform her own Region and you will follow with a short tour, meeting with the People, this time as their King."

"But I know the People will accept me," I said confidently. "This will be the beginning of a new era of comfort, a new era of equality, a new era of beauty," I mused, gesturing with my arms for emphasis.

Eden grinned, "That is good material for a speech. Save it for the People. But we will talk later. Come, your Governors await you, my King." Eden touched his hand to his forehead as a sign of respect and we both laughed as we walked arm in arm from my rooms and into the Great Hall where the Governors waited, their voices shouting to proclaim my arrival.

Segment 8

Tree-Stone

8

And so it happened that I became King of the world. Too easy, right? That's what I should have been thinking at the time, but instead I was caught up in the pageantry of the moment. As we'd decided, the Governors informed their Regions that I was to be ruler. From what the Governors told me the People's reaction was one of overwhelming approval for my new role. But I was still frightened—after all, I'd never been King before. A traveling prophet I knew how to be, that was easy, but a King....

While I was adjusting to my newly acquired power, I noticed that Eden was going through great lengths to propel his limitless energy plan out of the theoretical and into the practical, that is, he wanted to actually begin building and implementing Amaia in one of the Regions, with the idea that eventually all Regions would benefit by having their own. And I must say, the People were in love[1] with the idea. Of course, it was easy to accept Eden's plan simply on the basis of his word. He described the benefits unlimited power would bring to the People. He told them they could have devices to make their lives easier. The need to toil in the ground was a thing of the past, he said; we could produce and power machines that would do all the work, producing food for everyone. People would not become sick for lack of treatment because we could build such sophisticated equipment that any ailment would be cured. People would no longer suffer in sweltering homes, nor would they freeze during the cold months. Eden's energy machines would provide comfort during even the most unfavorable weather.

Eden also promised that if his machines were implemented we could travel at faster speeds. The ancient beltways would be a thing of the past, giving way to sleek, efficient, and fast transport options. The world would become smaller as people could travel through the united Regions freely and without cost or effort. Which reminds me of his most attractive promise, to create such a wealth of power that units would no longer be needed. How he intended to accomplish this I was not sure and, to be honest, I did not altogether approve of him making this claim. But it was my job now to ensure the People went along with the plan, so I embarked on my first tour as King.

With Eden's work preceding me my tours were more successful than ever, with multitudes congregating to welcome me as their King. And from what I saw, the People were ready for change. In every Region I saw them hurting. The Governors had wrung their people dry, squeezing every last drop of vitality from them. So for them, my becoming King was proof that their cries to Aigonz had been heard. I was heralded as a savior and Eden's Amaia was my chariot, carrying me into their hearts[2]. I believed we could make a change for the better. I wanted so much to make a change for all, to bring security and comfort to them, to show them the peace Aigonz brought to me.

And as expected, the People demanded their Governor build an Amaia as quickly as possible. So with the People satisfied, I ordered Amaia be built. This was my first action as King. I remember that day. I stood before the Governors, now united under a single currency, a single rule, and informed them the building of Eden's machines would commence. The sounds of approval echoed through the Great Hall, where I had assembled the Governors to be addressed. I announced the best place to start was in Nyanga, which would serve as the model for all future machines.

I finished addressing the Governors and took my seat among them to listen as Eden explained the finer points of providing limitless energy. Settling in my chair, I remember feeling confident and comfortable, even though my headdress was much too tall and my robes much too bright. But these were all signs of my new position, I told myself. I remember not really listening to Eden as he explained how the machines would be built; I was more caught up in the excitement of seeing all our plans coming to fruition. I thought about how the People loved me, worshiped me, about how wonderful our world would be when we were free from the grip of corruption, greed and vice. I though of all the wonderful things unlimited energy could produce for us, how we would never have a need for conflict or war. Our problems could be settled fairly, hard labor would be abolished, and the People would no longer spend their lives as slaves to the Nobles.

'All will be equal,' I thought, 'All will be free. Then all will have the opportunity to know Reality as I knew it to be, and with my guidance we could, collectively, reach a spiritual height never before known to humans. This will be the highest point of human evolution[3],' I mused. But my thoughts were interrupted when I heard Eden explaining how the machines were to be powered.

"Some of you have noticed that no machine can produce limitless energy, for all are powered using a substance which must eventually be replaced. I am here to say that limitless means Amaia can sustain a virtually boundless output of energy without ever needing to be recharged. The only substance capable of meeting these requirements is the rare element called Tree-stone. But Tree-stone is very difficult to obtain, and it is clear there is not enough Tree-stone within the boundaries of our great land to power even one Amaia. This is why we must enter into the Forgotten Land and take the plentiful Tree-stone that is available there."

Tree-stone. Of course! I'd forgotten this was the source of power for Amaia and was found in abundance in the Forgotten Land. Eden continued, "The savages of this land will surrender their property to us easily. They are a strange and backward people, living by ancient methods and worshiping antiquated gods. They have not been able to enjoy the pleasures and comforts civilization[4] has to offer. The Forgotten People can be cruel and barbaric. They can be unforgiving and unreasonable. It is a great crime in their community to disturb the land, but they do not punish for crimes as we do. They do not have cages, they simply use words to punish those who offend. Do we fear words? Physical resistance is what we should fear, but words are no cause for alarm."

I stood when I heard this, looking up at Eden from my place among the Governors. "Is it right, though, for us to violate their laws for our own gain?" I said, appealing to my colleagues for support. "There must be another way." I did not like the idea of taking what we needed from the Forgotten People, especially if it involved committing a great crime in their society. Aigonz' law did not forbid disturbing the land, in fact it encouraged progress[5], but I still wanted some reassurance from Eden that this was the right thing to do.

"This is the only way to bring the relief the People demand," he said; "we will disturb the land the Forgotten People inhabit to obtain Tree-stone. You must understand, my friends, that Tree-stone is not easy to get to; it is not simply lying on the ground. The ground must be torn up, consumed[6] to find it, and even then it does not appear in abundance. We might find one small amount over a space the size of Nyanga city, and each Amaia will require double, perhaps triple this amount to continue running properly. This means that a very large quantity must be on hand at all times in order to power the number of Amaia we will build. Governors, the People have demanded Amaia be built. Our King has decreed it as well. The time for action is now."

There was a disturbance among the Governors when Eden said this. As I returned to my seat, Governor Hiru spoke up, "With respect to you, sir, and to our King, we ask how Amaia is to be funded? Where will the units come from to support such a huge project? We, the Governors, can not help in this regard; the units must come from elsewhere."

Eden was unaffected as he answered, "The People have demanded Amaia and so the People will fund its construction." Eden paused for a moment and glanced in my direction, knowing this was contrary to what we had discussed. Indeed, funding of the Amaia was something we decided should fall on the shoulders of the Governors. The People were without units to spare and the few they had were barely enough to keep them alive. So naturally, I was shocked that Eden said this, so different was it from our agreement.

I thought it my place to speak up, "How will the People fund this project when the People have nothing to begin with? It is already a losing endeavor if the People must be relied upon to build the machine. Surely, we as Nobles have more than enough units to fund the construction of Amaia. It will be completed easily and without problems; we will not even notice the units missing from our collections. We have so much already, why not give some of it back to those who need it?"

When I finished speaking those words a great tumult erupted among the Governors. A few stood and walked away, while others protested loudly against what I'd said. They insisted their collections were theirs and theirs alone and not to be redistributed for the sake of a machine, no matter how beneficial that machine may be. Eden's eyes narrowed and he turned his head to look at me. His look was different than any I'd seen from him before. I felt confused and frightened of him for the first time; this did not look like the man I knew. Worry must have shown on my face, because Eden quickly changed his expression to one of concern, furrowing his brows and giving me a private smile. When the Governors finished complaining among themselves and all had returned to their seats, Eden spoke again.

"I will fund the construction of the first Amaia, to be built here in Nyanga. Once the People see the wonders that come of it they will surrender their units without question. Plus, when they see that a Noble has enough trust in Amaia that he puts his own units into its construction they will surely fund more to be built." As he spoke I began to worry. Things were not going as I envisioned. But within myself, Aigonz urged me to move forward with Eden's plans, so I kept silent, intending to voice my objections to Eden in private.

The suggestion that Eden fund the first Amaia was instantly agreeable to the Governors. With that issue settled, the conversation shifted back to Tree-stone. "We have enough Tree-stone here and among the various Regions to provide power for the Nyanga Amaia," Eden said, "but more will be needed, and soon. This is why we must enter the Forgotten Land without delay and begin work to remove Tree-stone. The extraction process will cause us no difficulty, and the Forgotten People are not even worth thinking about. They are stupid and lazy and will not create a violent resistance as it is against their ways."

"But what of their laws?" I called out. "Surely they will resist when they find us violating their most sacredly held beliefs."

Eden laughed and answered confidently, "As I said before, there will be no resistance. The Forgotten People can only dance and chant to fight off threats, they can not pick up weapons against us. They will watch as we take what we need. They will pray to their useless gods as we move forward in the name of peace for our world. I know they will not resist, so it is good that we proceed as quickly as possible."

But it still felt wrong. Haven't we done enough taking in our world, I thought? Is it really appropriate to simply take what isn't ours, just because we want it? The Governors talked quietly to each other, all voicing their approval, but I was not satisfied. My emotions got the better of me and I jumped to my feet. "Let me talk to them!" I burst out. The room became silent as all eyes fixed on me. I stood and faced the Governors and Eden. "I will travel to the Forgotten Land and speak with its people directly. I will appeal to them to allow us to disturb their land. I will explain to them the importance of Treestone to us, how we need it to create peace and equality in our world."

Eden waved his arms at me, "It is a worthless endeavor, my friend. They will never agree."

"But I must try," I urged. "Perhaps I could invite them to join us in our new utopia. They will certainly benefit from moving out of their primitive state and into our world of comforts, of civilization." I became increasingly more excited as I spoke, realizing the possibilities in what I was saying. "I will speak to them of Aigonz and the wonderful things It does for us all. This will be the true joining of all people on earth, not just the Regions but everyone, equal and at peace." I beamed at the Governors, waiting for approval. To my surprise they appeared genuinely uninterested in what I had to say. Crestfallen, I looked at Eden for some gesture of approval.

"We certainly will not stand in your way, my King," Eden said, looking around at the Governor's skeptical expressions, "but you will find them to be unresponsive. The Forgotten People[7] have been forgotten by our world for a reason. They will not work with us; they are content to live in ignorance. But go, if you must, and we will remain here and begin construction in Nyanga."

"Yes, it will be so," I answered. "Please, my friends, respect your King and do not take any steps toward the Forgotten Land[8] until I return. I believe we can come to a solution that will be agreeable to everyone." I searched the Governor's faces for a reaction to tell me they agreed, but they simply shifted in their seats and gave each other sideways glances.

I took control of the meeting. "Then let it be so," I declared. "Edensaw, thank you for your efforts and hard work. This meeting has now ended. We will not meet again until after my return. Again, do not proceed into the Forgotten Land without my consent, as you love your King you must also obey. Now go, my friends." The Governors formed little huddles, talking privately amongst themselves and slowly filtered out of the room. I approached Eden and requested his private attention. "I expected you to want my attention," he smiled.

"Let us walk together," I said. "There is much we need to discuss."

At first we strolled in silence, arm in arm. My mind raced with doubts and confusion, wondering if we were about to commit a terrible error. We entered the garden, our feet rustling through the emerald lawn, and stopped beneath the Dheal tree, the very place where we first shared each other. It was in the shade of the tree that I broke our quiet. "Eden, I don't know if this is right. If the Forgotten People do not agree to give us their Tree-stone I can not permit its taking. Even though they will not resist, it would be wrong to take what is not ours. Is there another option?" My voice shook and tears began to well in my eyes as Eden stopped walking and turned me about to face him.

He wiped the liquid from my face with his thumbs and put his lips to my forehead. "Everything will be alright, my companion," he whispered. "You are the master of diplomacy and a true Prophet. The Forgotten People will be foolish not to agree to help us and more foolish still to remain in their primitive land."

I put my ear to his chest. His heart was beating quickly but his demeanor was calm as always. "But you said they would not. If they do not give us Tree-stone we must find another option."

I looked at him for some small reassurance. Eden brushed the hair from my face and grinned, "I will do everything in my power to find a solution while you are gone. I promise you no harm will come of this, only prosperity, only progress."

His voice was reassuring but I was not consoled. Something was wrong, I could feel it. "Eden, please leave me. I want to be alone," I said, trembling with emotion. Eden nodded and released me from his embrace. He placed his hand on his forehead. "My King, my companion, do what you feel is right." He walked back toward the Great Hall, leaving me to my thoughts. The day was bright and warm in the garden, but I collapsed shivering under the Dheal tree and wept bitterly, crying out to Aigonz for release[9] from my burden.

Segment 9

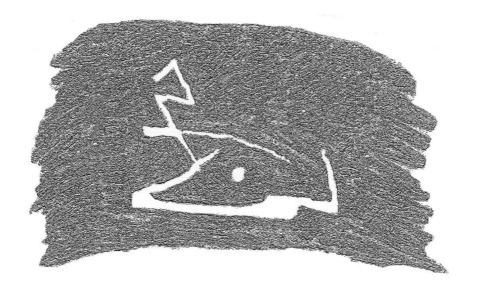

Mapu

9

As I was resting moments ago I was thinking about how resilient the human body can be. I've been down here for what seems like days and I'm still alive. I haven't had a drop of water or a scrap of food since the door was shut, yet I can still write these words. But death is becoming a reality to me now. I admit I've already tried to open the door, but of course it will not budge. I've attempted to eat my clothes but they're no relief. My hand trembles even as I press these symbols into shape. My entire body is on fire from lack of water. But I will continue, I must continue, for your sake, for the sake of the world, yours and those to come. It's important that I finish[1].

When I last wrote I was describing my intention to visit the Forgotten Land. Now, little was known in my world of the Forgotten Land except where it was. There was plenty of land on the planet during my age but a large amount of it was covered in ice. What was left was claimed as property of the Regions, with the exception of the Forgotten Land, which began at the border of the most remote Region, known as Kurrurbun.

Now, this Kurrurbun was located in a place that was not ideal for supporting life. Most of the main city was built up inside a pocket of sand, a small desert really, protected by looming dunes known to creep into the city and cause problems for its inhabitants. The surrounding land wasn't much different, with areas of soil intermingled with powdery desert. Food was difficult to produce because what soil was there was rocky and plant life had trouble growing, making it hard to keep animals. But as inhospitable as it was, people still thrived in Kurrurbun. Beyond its borders, however, the land became increasingly less forgiving. Living in this mysterious place was a society, a very ancient people about whom almost nothing was known. Of course, these were who I sought, who we named the Forgotten People.

I reached Kurrurbun easily enough and stopped to charge my transport and gain information from the locals about how to find the Forgotten People. One man was particularly helpful, giving me landmarks and pointing me in a general direction. He also warned me that the Forgotten People were not to be trusted and I must be cautious when dealing with them. He told me they took part in strange and blasphemous[2] rituals and were capable of superhuman feats. They could kill a person just by looking at her, the man said, and they could change their form to appear as one of us. I listened to all he said and thanked him, wondering if there could actually be some truth behind his warnings.

My stay in Kurrurbun was short, and I was soon on my way beyond the boundaries of my world. As I watched the last of the city fade into the landscape behind me, I began thinking about Eden. It occurred to me that he retained a significant amount of information about these people and the land they inhabited. To know that much about the Forgotten People was unusual, especially for someone who wasn't raised as a Noble. But, I reasoned, he needed to power Amaia and so had researched the best places to find Tree-stone. Plus, Kurrurbun was his home city and, having lived there, he would have more knowledge about the Forgotten People than most.

As I glided along I kept all of this in my mind. My transport was equipped to run for months without recharging and it was a good thing too, for I really had no idea where I needed to go. The land was becoming less hospitable than in Kurrurbun, and I wondered to myself how any civilization could survive under these conditions. The soil was a red-brown color with sparse, struggling vegetation dotting the landscape. Hills rose in the distance, small, ancient, and covered in rocks, with squat trees adorning their shallow crowns. As I continued through the unexplored countryside I could see in the distance a great chasm in the earth, as if the ground had split in two, creating a fissure so long and deep that when I approached it to investigate I could barely see the bottom.

But the most noticeable difference was the temperature. The further away from my world I traveled the warmer it became. Now, I was making this trip during the warm months and the heat in the Forgotten Land was almost unbearable. The air was so stifling, in fact, that I removed most of my robes and traveled only in my most basic under-clothing.

Following the man's directions I soon came upon a large stone structure. The building seemed uninhabited and looked as though it was as old as the landscape. I stopped my transport and stepped out into the soil to investigate. The structure had been created using many small, rectangular objects, hard as rock to the touch but much too uniform to be natural. 'These must have been made by human hands,' I thought.

The bricks were the same color as the ground and I surmised they were created using the dirt itself, fashioned and stacked one atop the other, one next to the other, creating a continuous grid so tightly interlocked even a blade of grass could not fit between them. In fact, I remember thinking that if I poured water into the building it would hold every drop with no leaks anywhere. The walls were smooth to the touch and there were many different decorations along the top portion of the building. This was unlike anything I had ever seen. It reminded me of buildings people in my world once created, but ours were made from wood or naturally occurring rock. Such building materials were ancient by my world's standards, as our cities had been constructed almost exclusively from metal.

Seeing there was no one around I left the strange

structure and continued traveling along the route the man in Kurrurbun recommended. It wasn't long before I noticed an oasis in the distance supporting trees, green vegetation and a water source. From my transport I could see three women tending to some animals and loading containers full with the fruits of the oasis. I knew then I'd found the first of those I sought.

Their animals were tall and gangly, with blankets covering their arched backs. The women stopped what they were doing and turned to watch me as my transport glided to meet them. They were hardly clothed, with strips of cloth wrapped about their tan waists and nothing more, and they clutched woven baskets at their hip. The women had dark skin and short dark hair, neatly fastened with small restraints and were barefoot but showed no signs of discomfort despite the incredibly hot climate.

Amazing, I thought. I'd traveled only a very short distance outside of the most remote Region in my world and discovered the Forgotten People closer than I ever thought. They were right there, the whole time, so near, like a memory you know is there but just can't catch. I was delighted to find that they were all very beautiful as well, smiling at me with snow-white teeth as I climbed from my transport and walked toward them. The women placed their baskets on the ground and walked to meet me. Approaching them, I was naturally cautious, especially considering all the warnings I received about the Forgotten People. But they did not seem dangerous at all. In fact, I quickly discovered they were more than gracious hosts.

I stopped in front of the women and spoke slowly, hoping they would understand. "Hello, friends. I am visiting from the city of Kurrurbun. Do you understand me?"

The women giggled to themselves and one replied, "Yes, friend, of course we understand you." Her voice was like music, much different from the way we spoke in my world but unmistakably accurate nonetheless. "Welcome to our land. We seldom receive visitors from the outside world." I laughed to myself that they considered my world, with its grand cities and massive luxuries, to be on the outside.

I continued, "I have traveled a great distance to find you and your people. Tell me, what are you?"

"I am a woman, can't you tell?" she said, holding up her arms and spinning around on her toes. The three laughed at her answer, and I did as well. "Yes, I can tell you're a woman. What I meant was, what is the name of your people? To what group do you belong?"

"My people do not have a group apart from another group. We are all the same. We are Tlinee[3]."

"I have never heard of the Tlinee people before," I said. "Are you related to any other groups I may be more familiar with?"

Again the woman looked puzzled. "We are not 'the Tlinee people,' we are Tlinee only. There is no other name but Tlinee."

Now it was my turn to be confused. "In my world people have been split into groups," I said. "If a person came from Nyanga she is called Nyangan, or 'from the Region of Nyanga.' If one is from Kurrurbun she is called Kurrurbunian. Is this not the same for your world?"

"We are Tlinee, that is all," was her answer. She looked at me with an air of bewildered pleasure as I silently wrestled with her description. "Well, you do have a name, don't you?" I asked.

She laughed, "Yes, I have a name. I am called Eskarne[4]."

I introduced myself and asked where I might find their city. One of the other women spoke up. "We have a large settlement not too far from here. We will take you there, if

119

you have come in peace." Her voice was warm but firm, implying that anything but peace would not get me very far with them.

"It is peace that I seek from you, my friends, for my world has found itself in need. I have come to make a great request of your people and your land; the Tlinee are the only ones who can help us."

The woman pursed her lips and replied, "We know nothing of such things, but we can take you to one who can help. We are here merely to harvest some of the tender shoots that grow around the spring this time of year. But we have all we need and can take you to our home if you will follow us."

"I would like that very much," I replied. The women hoisted their baskets and supplies from the ground and fixed them onto the backs of the animals. I watched with curiosity as they shouted a command, pulling on ropes attached to the animal's heads, prompting them to rise up from their rest. Once the animals were up and walking the women held the ropes and used them to pull the animals along next to them. What a wonderful partnership, beasts and people. While we in my world were creating machines to do our work, these women could simply ask an animal to do it and they seemed willing to oblige. This was something I'd never seen before, animals doing work for people.

I returned to my transport and followed behind them slowly, staying far enough away so not to scare the beasts[5], who eyed my vehicle with careful suspicion as they lumbered forward. As we traveled, above the hum of my engines, I could hear the women singing with each other, a song that flowed with their motion and felt to me as old as the hills themselves.

Our little caravan moved slowly through the desert and it was not long before I saw smoke on the horizon. From a sandy hilltop, one of the women motioned to me and pointed to a valley just below us, as if to indicate we'd reached our destination. As we descended a rocky trail I could see the valley was actually quite vast and well-concealed by the mountains that claimed its border, stretching farther into the horizon than I could see. A vibrant green gleamed from the land, still half hidden from view by a fine mist that floated like a cloud above the fertile soil.

Drawing closer, dwellings appeared among the lush plant life and massive trees below, but were still too far away to look like anything more than small huts and isolated fires. Our approach saw the arid, sandy ground yield to moist, fertile land. Rivers and streams materialized, cutting through the dirt, carrying life with them to this unexpected garden in the midst of the desert. It was very much like the gardens in Nyanga, I thought, but much larger, maybe as large as Nyanga itself.

As I daydreamed, we reached level ground and drifted into a thick forest, dense but for the clearings cut beside the road. We continued through the forest for a short time until we came upon a small river, with a group of huts gathered along its bank, the same dwellings I'd seen from above. The women walked closer to the huts and tied their animals to a post, giving them fresh water and food as they did.

I stopped, exited my transport and surveyed the area. The road we were traveling seemed to turn away from the river and continue back into the forest. I peered down the road and was surprised to see a child standing in the middle, looking directly at me. The child, realizing she was discovered, disappeared from the road, into the forest. I started toward her but stopped short when people began pouring from the woods, from all directions, gathering around me and inspecting my vehicle. Some eyed me suspiciously, but most seemed delighted I was there. 'These look like healthy, happy people,' I thought, not the ruthless savages I'd created in my mind. As they continued to come out of the forest I realized where I was. This was not another winding road through the forest but the entrance to a great village, a sprawling community carved out of the landscape, blending with the contours of the valley to create a spectacular symbiosis between people and nature. I'd found the village of the Forgotten People.

Eskarne approached me through the crowd that had gathered, taking my arm and leading me away from the river and into the village itself. Earthen and animal skin huts were scattered about in no real order except that they created well swept, hard-dirt roadways on which the Forgotten People traversed. Each dwelling was nestled between trees so large that in some instances they composed the majority of the house. There were many people milling about, but when they saw me they stopped what they were doing and stared. I was impressed with myself. Even here I was famous, I thought, although for what reason I did not know.

The Forgotten People all had a similar light brown skin-tone, no doubt caused by their constant exposure to the extreme heat. They all wore little clothing, young and old, but seemed completely comfortable in their state of undress. Some of the men sat cross-legged behind large rocks, grinding pieces of metal into sharp points or quietly smoking pipes. Women carried water in clay jars balanced on their heads as their children ran and played alongside, the smallest ones perched on their mother's backs, held fast with cloth wrappings.

"Do not mind the stares of my friends," Eskarne said. "Most have never seen your kind before, but we have heard a great deal about you. We know you live in a place far from us, a place that does not pray[6] to the land, a place that wounds the land and destroys the sacred[7] mountains to build cities of iron. This describes your home, yes?"

"Yes," I answered, surprised at her accuracy, "that is

my home. But we have realized the error of our ways and have decided to make a change for the better. That is why I am here, to seek the guidance of your people, to help us create a better world for everyone. We have devised a great machine that will put an end to your labor, will create great comforts for all to enjoy, and will remove the need for war." I stopped and smiled at Eskarne, who squinted her eyes in confusion at my prediction.

"But here, in Mapu[8], we do not fear labor," she said, "for there is not much labor to be done. We take what the land gives us, we eat when an animal gives his life for us, and we never go hungry. We have enough for all and share equally so no one is left without. Look around you, look at the space we have to move our bodies and grow food. Sometimes the air blows cold and frosts cover the ground, but we simply store food to eat during those times. We have lived here longer than any can recall. We know that the Tlinee have lived here since the beginning of time, before even the ice began to take hold, when the mist that covers this valley canopied the entire earth. And as for comforts," she laughed, "we have many. Come, look inside my dwelling."

Eskarne halted our slow stroll through the village in front of a hut, the outer walls fashioned from fretted animal skins wrapped around four large trees, forming a unique shape with its thick insulated covering. Inside was indeed a pleasure for the senses, brightly decorated with an artistry the likes of which I'd never seen before. Depictions of men hunting great woolen beasts covered one wall, while love scenes were portrayed on the other. People entwined, man, woman, all combinations, sharing pleasurable and loving encounters, shown here as simply a part of their life, with no negativity attached, only joyous looks on the faces of the participants. This type of art would have been a disgrace in my world, but here it seemed perfectly natural.

The hut itself was quite large, perhaps 16 Redetrad (in all), a size comparable to that of my own rooms, which were considered large by any standard. The floor was covered in a moss-like grass that was not stiff and prickly but rather soft and forgiving when trod upon, and cool on my feet. Flaps opened at the top of the hut, allowing sunlight and air inside, but easily closed in case of rain or cold. Although the heat of the Forgotten Land was for me nearly unbearable, beneath the tree-canopy and inside Eskarne's hut the temperature was quite comfortable, so effective was the animal-skin covering. On one side of the hut there were gathered a number of different beds, each consisting of thick animal fur and set at a different level, with a wooden platform holding it off the ground.

"How many people live in this dwelling, Eskarne?" I asked my guide.

"Me and my husband and our children, and that is all," she said. "However, many times friends or relatives will stay as well, and we may enjoy the same comforts in their dwelling places. Everything is for all to use, so we find no discomfort when a visitor wishes to share our accommodations."

'Very strange,' I thought to myself. In my world, we lived for the benefit of individual gain and the pursuit of private property. It was the goal of a person in my world to increase the amount of units she had so she might obtain comforts for herself and none other. Some had been known to share, but only with the most trusted and close acquaintances and even then with a certain amount of guarded apprehension.

I stepped from the hut and absorbed the village around me. Children laughed and tumbled about, men and women interacted with smiles and friendly gestures. No one was broken from debt or causing conflict or swinging in a cage, empty and defeated. "What do the Tlinee do with those who break the law?" I asked Eskarne.

"We do not have criminals here," she said. "There have

been times when people have done things that violate our way of life. When this happens we decide as a community how the situation is to be handled. Almost always a resolution can be reached and the offender is taught that what he has done is wrong and how to avoid similar misdeeds in the future. This usually works well, in part because we are constantly reminded of what is right and what is wrong."

"How are you reminded?" I asked.

Eskarne looked up and pointed to the mountains that surrounded the fertile rift they had claimed as their home. "These mountains tell us. They hold for us our stories, they remind us of the right way to act. There are spirits[9] that live in these mountains and they keep our laws for us. We must always remember the lessons the land has taught us. Then we can point to the mountain and say, 'Never forget The-Tree-That-Was-Broken[10],' and nothing more. Then the lesson is been taught, reinforced, and Tlinee obey, for we know the stories are there to help us."

"But what happens when someone still commits wrongdoing despite the stories and council of others?" I pressed.

Eskarne looked down at the ground, her eyes welling with sadness. "This has only happened once in my lifetime. That person was asked to leave Mapu and never return. That person was my brother." I could see my question had stirred an unpleasant emotion within her and I quickly decided to abandon the issue. I admit, at the time I did not have a good idea of what Eskarne was saying. As far as my experience went, mountains and trees could not talk at all, let alone tell stories. 'Well, they are primitives,' I thought, 'and this is probably an example of what Eden meant when he said they were unreasonable and backward, worshiping ancient gods that have long since died out.' But I could not ignore the reason for my visit.

"Eskarne, do your people have a leader? Someone I can talk to about matters that affect both your world and mine?

She smiled and said, "Of course, you mean Kuthula[11]. This is the one I told you could help. He is over this way. Follow me please." Eskarne escorted me past many huts that were similar to her own, but each in its own way unique, and led me to the middle of what was a cluster of dwellings, creating a perimeter around a small central hut that seemed to be an extension of the ground, its walls composed entirely of earth. A wrinkled old man sat outside of the center hut, cross-legged on the ground, drawing pictures in the dust with a large sturdy stick, a doleful expression on his worn face. When Eskarne approached he looked up and, rising painfully, hobbled over to meet us.

The man appeared to be very old and looked as though he'd been weathered by the elements themselves. A gray beard covered his mouth and chin but the sides of his face were clean and hairless. His skin was darker than most others and his eyes were deep and brown but sparkling with knowledge. I could tell this was their leader just by his presence, which emanated a pure projection of kingship. This was someone who has earned his position, I thought, not bought or inherited it.

"I have been waiting a long time for you to come," the old man said to me, covering the top of his stick with his hands and resting his chin on them. His voice was like a bird's song, not worn like the elders of my world but clear and pure, unwavering and filled with vigor.

I was taken aback at his words, for I thought the Forgotten People knew nothing of my world. As I tried to formulate a reply we locked gazes. His eyes were searching mine, for what I was not sure, but I felt as though he could look into my mind, into my intentions, and grasp immediately what my motives were. I stammered, "How did you know

I was coming?" The old man lifted his head from his cane and said, "Please follow me. Eskarne, you have done well by bringing this guest among the Tlinee. Now, return to your pleasures."

Eskarne softly squeezed my shoulder, turned, and walked back toward her hut. The old man bade me walk with him and we ambled slowly to his dwelling. He invited me in and closed the flaps behind us. "Please sit, my friend," he said, motioning to a comfortably shaped couch which was the only furnishing to be found inside.

"I have come a great distance to seek your help," I said to the man as he positioned himself facing me on the soft ground, his cane resting across his lap.

"Yes, I know you have. All my life I have known you would come. One such as yourself came to my ancestors and one such as yourself will return again in the distant future," the man said, a look of sadness in his eyes.

I was puzzled. "I do not understand. How can you know the future?"

"Have no fears, all will be revealed to you. Your intentions are pure, but your world, I'm afraid, is doomed. The earth will survive but must withstand another great turmoil before all is returned to balance[12]." The old man settled himself and looked upward, toward the sky. "My name is Kuthula, and I will tell you everything you seek and perhaps some knowledge you did not know you sought." He chuckled softly, as if he'd just told a joke. I sat quietly on the couch as Kuthula began to talk, our conversation, which was supposed to be about Tree-Stone, had already taken a much different path.

"We are Tlinee, as you have already discovered." His voice dipped and soared as he spoke. "Your world has given us the name Forgotten, but this name has meaning only to those who can not remember. We have lived in this place before the ice shelves formed, before the sun scorched the land, before your ancestor's ancestors built their cities. Tlinee have lived on the land since the beginning of people and we have not forgotten this history. Tlinee have survived on earth through each cycle of ice and thaw, our stories unchanged and our knowledge the most ancient that has survived. We have endured countless destructions, countless climate changes, countless shifts in the earth's stability. We have seen fire rain from the sky, we have shivered as war-clouds darkened the sun's warmth. Tlinee have lived separate from others who chose to venture forth from this land in search of wealth and property to keep for themselves alone, those who have denied the way of life we here enjoy."

"But this is why I have come," I said, "to bring all the people of the world together. My world has decided to live peacefully, to reject the greed and individualism of our past and unite under a single rule. I am their King. I commune with Aigonz and It has told me it is right to come here and offer to the Tlinee a chance to enjoy a life of bliss, of unlimited power."

Kuthula smiled softly and replied, "I know in your heart you believe this to be true, but you have been deceived, I'm afraid."

Shock-waves ran though my limbs and heat tingled in my cheeks. I laughed nervously, even as my body sunk. "Deceived? No, my friend, I am certain I have not. Aigonz would have told me if this were true."

"Do not mistake Aigonz' voice with individual duty, my friend. What is right for one may not be right for all. It was your duty to become King, to listen to the advice of others, and to come here in search of my aid."

My eyes opened wide and I stared at Kuthula in stunned silence. "Again, do not fear my knowledge of your world, my friend. It has happened this way before and will again. Unfortunately, once more, another age is drawing to its conclusion, another cycle is complete. You are here to ask for our land, or perhaps what lies beneath our land, to incorporate into a machine you believe will solve the problems of your world. Is this true?"

All I could do was agree, amazed that he knew so much. "Yes, I admit you are correct."

"Know this: those who are closest to you are your deceivers. They have used you to further their hidden plans, to create for themselves a world in which they own the land, the people, and everything else. They have devised a plan to take power from the land, not only for machines but for their own heights as well."

"I cry to Aigonz this is not true," I said.

"This is true, but the fault is not yours. Indeed, it could have been no other way for you. It is your duty to destroy the land, it is your duty to destroy your people, just as it is your duty to be here, now, and do as I instruct you."

The old man watched me as I rose from the couch and walked back and forth in front of him. I was becoming more upset with the idea that I was responsible for destroying my people. I could hear the voice of Yarakai Kartavya screaming at me, 'You will kill us all!' from his restraints in Quarantine. All I could think was, why was this happening to me? Why when all I wanted was to help?

"This is happening to you because it could not happen any other way," Kuthula said solemnly, reading my thoughts.

"I don't understand," I said. "I can choose to live any way I want, to create any outcome I desire. Is this not the case?"

"It is."

"Then why, when I choose to do right, am I told it will cause harm to others, innocents?"

"Because you are doing right by harming others,"

Kuthula said. "This is your duty. You have chosen to accomplish your duty, which is good. But good, when it has been squeezed dry, when it has been stretched so thin it is transparent, may take the appearance of evil before it can manifest in positive ways."

I crossed my arms and shook my head back and forth, "I do not understand."

"Please relax and listen," Kuthula said calmly, gesturing for me to return to my couch, a warm smile blooming on his lips. I obliged and sat back down, wiping my face and regaining my composure.

After a moment's pause, Kuthula continued, his dark eyes gleaming with silver as he spoke. "There are elements that exist in the world, everyone's world, that continually pass through us. We call these elements Viria. Viria have existed since the beginning of the world, since the beginning of time, since the beginning of humans, and are found in everything, everywhere. These elements are invisible to the naked eye, invisible even to the scientist's machines, but interact with people more than you know. The elements in question exist as two types, either positive or negative, or for you, good or bad. Viria collect within a larger piece of matter and sometimes cause it to have certain experiences based on the amount of either positive or negative that has accumulated."

"Wait," I interrupted, "I do not understand. Does this mean that, say, a rock or a tree or the clothes on my back hold these invisible elements?"

"Yes, that is correct," he nodded. "Viria pass through objects, collect within objects, and travel about seeking a place to congregate. Now, it so happens that pieces of matter like rocks or clothing may not be affected by a small amount of Viria because these things in fact have no emotion to affect. Humans, on the other hand, are prone to be influenced by the smallest presence of Viria in their bodies. But unlike a rock or a piece of clothing, a human has the ability to accept either type of Viria according to his individual circumstance."

"What does this mean, individual circumstance?" I asked.

"What I mean by this is that every human has lived on earth before."

"I don't remember living any other life but the one I'm living right now."

"And well you shouldn't," Kuthula replied. "These other lives were not lived by the person you call yourself or the person I think myself to be, but by the person whose reflection you can't see in a mirror[13], whose limbs cannot be broken, whose body cannot die. This person we Tlinee call Djin[14]. This person travels from physical bodies like ours to other bodies in the future, performing duties required of it or ignoring those duties in favor of its own desires."

"So you're saying my body[15] is not really me?" I asked.

"Your body is only an instance of your true self, a manifestation, a vehicle through which a certain duty must be performed. To perform the duty assigned to one's body is to do good. To ignore one's duty is to do wrong."

"So how do Viria work into this?"

Viria are present to assist a body with its duty," Kuthula answered. "A body is born with a propensity, a predisposition, a tendency to hold a certain amount of positive or negative Viria. So a body that has been born with the predisposition to receive much positive and little negative can choose to do so. That body will hold on to positive, gain it through the atmosphere, and release negative to others whose bodies require negative. Other bodies are predisposed to receiving negative Viria, changing, then returning them as positive; we call these people transformers[16]. "

I was quite confused, and at first a little skeptical, but

any doubts I had seemed to wash away as quickly as they surfaced. And though I inexplicably found myself absorbing this new world view, it was not entirely clear to me upon first listen.

"Just a moment, please. How does the atmosphere contain Viria and how do we receive it?" I asked.

"The atmosphere is really just the air around you, the air you breathe. And it is by this method that the most amount of Viria are received by the body. There is a small amount of Viria that enter through other means, but the primary entrance and exit point is through the breath. It is true that every living thing is breathing, always taking something in, always letting something out. If a body happens to enter into a space where there is a large concentration of negative Viria for example, that body has the opportunity to breath those Viria in, and almost all will. Now it is up to the body what it does with them.

"Many bodies in your world will hold on to negative Viria and exhale positive, for each body must contain a capacity at all times. That capacity can be purely negative, purely positive, or a mixture of both in any proportion. But remember, in some situations a body's predisposition can be challenged through the exercise of free choice, though not all bodies in your world have the capacity for free choice. However, it is ideal for a body to be predisposed to and subsequently contain pure positive, for at that point a body will experience the best possible life. In an ideal world, this can be achieved by every-body, but few realize this fact.

"Consider a situation where a person finds himself in a heightened emotional state. Extreme happiness, let's say. What happens when a person is extremely happy? That person will laugh. What is laughter other than the expulsion of breath, large amounts of breath, from the body? This is the expulsion of negative Viria back into the atmosphere. Now let us assume there are others in the room laughing also. There should then be a large amount of negative Viria collected in that space, correct?"

"Yes," I agreed, "That seems likely. But do the people not breath in the negative Viria that had just been eliminated?"

"The answer is two-fold," said Kuthula. "Most in fact do breath back negative Viria, but this is because they seek it. Either their bodies are predisposed to do so or they have chosen to occupy their capacity with negative Viria. But that aside, imagine with me the feeling of laughing. Tell me, how does it make you feel to laugh?"

"It makes me feel good to laugh," I said.

"Yes. That feeling is not always your body receiving positive Viria but expelling negative Viria. You see, when the negative have been removed the positive are most readily present and so the body feels the effects of these particles flowing through it. Now imagine yourself crying. The same mechanism is in place when the body expels bursts of breath. A person may be crying out of sadness but eventually it is the crying, the expulsion of breath, and in this case tears as well, that will make a person feel better. In fact, so connected are these two reactions that a person may even cry while he is laughing. If a person denies his urge to cry he will store more negative Viria than his body can handle and will suffer because of it. So we find that laughing and crying are almost completely alike and both result in the body removing excess negative that has been absorbed and stored. But this good feeling will fade if a body chooses or is predisposed to replenish its capacity with negative Viria."

I began to understand, "So if a person is somehow able to keep her positive Viria in a greater proportion at all times she would experience a feeling of great bliss, just because her body is filled with positive Viria."

Kuthula tapped his cane on the ground, "Yes, this is

correct. But few are able to remain in such a state, especially when positive is consumed by those whose bodies do not need an over-abundance. Many bodies, especially in the world you have traveled here from, consume far more positive than they need, leaving little for those who do need it. As a result, bodies exist whose duty it is to absorb and hold large amounts of negative Viria so the little positive that is left may be distributed among those who use it sparingly."

"This is what you meant when you said that certain bodies are predisposed to holding large amounts of negative, that it can be no other way for them," I said.

"Yes, this is true. Because of the Misaru[17] of their past bodies, they must perform the duty of retaining negative Viria for the duration of their life."

Just as quickly as I understood him I was lost again and needed more explanation. "Kuthula, what is Misaru?" I asked.

"Misaru is a balance, a system through which all things that are good and all things that are evil are kept at a constant equilibrium. During a body's time on earth the Djin is affected by the actions of the body. Now, each body is born with a certain duty to perform, that is, to collect and hold its capacity of positive or negative Viria. When a body performs its duty to the fullest and then dies, the Djin is able to return into a body which is predisposed to receive positive Viria and an advanced ability to retain them."

"Kuthula, will you please give me an example?" I requested.

"I will use terms from your world so you will understand. Imagine a Noble who lives his life in comfort, with no need to work, many friends and happy memories to bide the time. It can be said that this person has earned the opportunity to retain a large amount of positive Viria and so feels good much of the time. This is his duty because he has earned it based

134

on his Misaru. Now consider the person who, no matter what he does, is constantly faced with hardship, struggle. He may be stricken with disease, his plans to improve his comfort level may always fail, he may always do what he feels is right but seldom if ever reaps a positive feeling. This, too, is his duty. Because of his Misaru, he must retain large amounts of negative Viria because his body is predisposed to do so."

"But why should people live in pain?" I asked. "Is it not possible for a body to overcome its predisposition? Could not a body experience whatever amount of positive or negative it chooses?"

"Yes, this is not only possible, this is what we find happening in your world. Because people are choosing to absorb and retain disproportionate amounts of positive Viria, their gluttony throws the balance off, leaving a huge amount of negative unclaimed. This negative Viria must go somewhere, and for now it is only affecting people's bodies."

"How does this happen?"

"Recall a person who lives his life surrounded by pain, always pain, never pleasure."

My murderer, Yarakai Kartavya, was a perfect example. "Yes, I know the kind," I answered.

"These people are actually doing us a justice by accepting all the negative that has not been cared for. Since there is such a small amount of positive left, negative is thrust upon a body that is predisposed to receive it. So while many retain large amounts of positive, a few must retain significant amounts of negative in order to keep the balance. This is an example of good appearing as evil, for good will result for many when these bodies accept evil."

"And what happens when there aren't enough bodies left to absorb and retain the excess negative?" I asked.

Kuthula's face grew long, sadness filling his warm eyes. "You will receive the answer to that question very soon.

135

Your world has run out of bodies. Already, as we speak, those who once held the massive amounts of negative left by the indulgent few are choosing to ignore their duties and seek positive in excess. This means the huge amount of negative Viria left will have nowhere else to go but back to the earth. Once this happens...." The old man bowed his head and sighed, sorrow wearing his face thin.

But I was eager to know the end of his story. "Kuthula, what happens?" I asked cautiously.

"The same thing that happened to your ancestors, the same thing that happened to their ancestors and so on back to the beginning of humans."

I squinted my eyes at him, perplexed by his reticence. "My new friend," he said, "the earth is very ancient. It has existed longer than any human dare guess. During its time it has hosted many different forms of life; some have survived, some have disappeared. But humans are the one form that have not only survived but have time and again risen to dominate all other life.

"Humans have been able to master survival in the harshest of conditions using nothing more than their intellect. We have gone beyond using the earth for survival and procreation to seeking pleasure from it, recreation, leisure. But humans are a peculiar species. We have the ability to recognize how much we need yet still choose to use beyond our needs. Take a dog, for example. A dog will eat until it's stomach is so full it cannot fit any more food into it. Then it will purge the food only to continue eating again to excess. The dog cannot recognize that it has the choice to stop eating once it reaches its limit and so it continues eating. Humans, on the other hand, can recognize the choice to stop eating, to stop consuming, yet ignore that choice and yield to a most basic instinct—to consume beyond the body's limit to contain. The people of your world have devised a machine that will allow them to consume past the point of need, past the point of desire even, to a fullness that must then be purged."

"And you said this has happened before?" I asked, horrified by what I was hearing.

Kuthula rose from the ground and motioned to me to do the same. "Come with me. I have something to show you," he said, taking my arm and leading me from his hut. We walked back through the village. With the mountains behind us, we crossed the river and walked for some distance through an ever less fertile landscape, the lush forest thinning in favor of squat shrubbery. Finally, we came to a large field, rocky and cleared of trees, dusted with struggling plant life. Kuthula pointed toward a small stone wall in the distance, a structure not even half my height. "This is where we are going." His serious demeanor broke for a moment as we approached the wall, which I realized was actually an enclosure surrounding a fairly large pit in the earth. Upon closer inspection, I saw it housed not a pit but a staircase, a staircase that descended deep into the earth.

Kuthula turned to face me, a solemn expression preceding his words. "This place is the most sacred of all on earth for the Tlinee. This is called The Place of Hope. It is here you will return. Very soon, you will return." He shook his head mournfully as we stood on the top of the stairs, looking down into its blackness.

Startled by his words I asked, "Why must I return here? What business do I have in this place?"

Kuthula turned his head and stared straight into my eyes, "You have been chosen to tell the story of another human destruction."

"What do you mean, another human destruction?" I asked.

He sighed and sat on the top step, urging me to join him. We sat side by side, peering down the stairs and into the blackness below. "Your world is not the first on earth to build cities. Your world is not the first to establish a system of currency. Your world is not the first to devise machines and to master the use of unfiltered energy. And your world will not be the first to destroy itself."

"How can this be?" I wondered aloud.

"There was a time before your ancestors built their first city that the earth was covered in ice. Humans survived this ice-period[18] but were forced to remain in a very small area in order to survive. But the earth began to warm and the ice receded, giving way to more land for humans to use. The remnants of this period still exist today, as the ice-shelves we consider a normal part of the earth's construction."

"The ice-shelves?" I said. "They once covered the earth?"

"Yes, but this is during recent times, years before your birth, but a small time compared to how old the earth is. There was also an age when the ice shelves were not there, when the earth was much warmer and there was very little ice left. During this period much land was exposed and people roamed far across the earth."

"What happened to those people?" I asked.

"They chose to destroy themselves. They took more than the earth could give. They held more positive Viria than was available, and the earth was forced to purge them from existence."

"So when they absorbed positive Viria where did the negative Viria go?"

"The only place it could go," he answered, "into the earth itself. The earth is made of materials that serve as a passage for positive or negative Viria and it maintains a balance according to its own duty."

I was astounded. "The earth has a duty the same as people do?"

"It does, but the earth does not choose to obey or ignore its duty—it performs it without question. However, if it is forced to absorb Viria beyond its constant balance, the earth will react violently. Its only option will be to renew itself after such an imbalance is reached. For the earth this means a change to the landscape, but for the living things on earth it means destruction. Humans are the primary cause of the imbalance and so they are purged. Not all, for as you know humans still roam the earth, even after countless purge-cycles."

"So when this happens, why does the earth revert to an ice-period?"

Kuthula threw his hands up, "I do not know the answer to this. What I do know is that there have been many cycles of ice and thaw. During thaw periods, civilizations take root and grow across the earth. We are in a thaw period right now, just as we were many many times past, just as we will be many many times again. That is, unless people choose to end the cycle."

"But if people do not know they are repeating a cycle they may never change their behavior," I said.

"That is why we are here," said Kuthula, pointing to the steps leading into blackness. "These steps end in a place that will keep you safe long enough to record all that has happened in your world and will preserve your words for the people of the next thaw."

"What is this place?" I asked, starting down into the blackness. My voice echoed as I finished my sentence. I put my hand on the wall rising from the stairs and it felt like a material I had never before encountered, textured and rough to the touch but at the same time smooth.

"This place was built during a thaw, perhaps one of the first. It is ancient, going back as far as humans themselves. But it was created for one reason, and that is to endure no matter what disasters around it arise." Kuthula lifted his hands and gestured to our surroundings. "The land we are standing on at this moment was once submerged in water, was once burning with fire, was once as you see it now, and was once home to a great city much like your own. But these stairs, and the chamber that they lead to, have remained intact, unaffected by the earth's purging."

"How do the Tlinee know of such an ancient place?"

"Our stories tell us this. The story of these stairs and the chamber below has been passed among our people through many thaws, always preserving the original intention for this place to exist."

"And I am supposed to live down there until the disasters pass?" I asked, pointing into the dark.

He looked into my eyes, resting his gnarled hand on my shoulder. "No, my new friend, you are supposed to die there," Kuthula said.

I was overwhelmed with fear as I peered into the blackness that would become my tomb. "There must be another way, Kuthula. There is still hope for my world. I will take the knowledge you have given me here and warn the people, warn the Governors, that our world is soon to be destroyed. Everyone in my world trusts me and will do as I command. I am their King." I began to feel a sharp urge to leave immediately, to rush back to the Regions and herald my new wisdom.

Kuthula put his hand on my shoulder and turned me back toward the village. We walked away from the underground stairs and Kuthula spoke. "You will try to save them but they will not inderstand. Although you have only been gone a short time here in Mapu, you will return to a very different world than the one you left. You will try to warn them but they will not listen. They are too far gone."

I jumped from his embrace and stood in front of him,

"No, I don't believe you. There is good let for my people. They trust me to help them; they are certain to heed my warnings."

"Go, try to save them," Kuthula said. "But when the first of your energy machines begin to rupture, flee here, meet me again. I will be waiting for you."

Urgency rushed through me as I decided to leave the Forgotten Land and return to my world immediately. I bade Kuthula farewell and started back toward the river and my transport. I hadn't gone but a few steps when I heard him yelling after me. I turned to listen, and what he said shocked me. "My friend, go and tell all what you have heard here. But know this—there is one close to you who already knows the truths I have revealed to you today. He once lived among us, a Tlinee, but chose to ignore the truth. He used his knowledge to create machines. You know this man, my friend. He was given the name Edensaw Megedagik Tasapainottaa."

Segment 10

Misaru

10

My transport hummed as I slid across the rocky terrain of Mapu. Eden, a Tlinee! Eden, a Forgotten Person! That explains why he knew so much about them, I thought. My mind raced back to our debate—there were so many of his arguments that coincided with what Kuthula said to me. 'How could he keep this a secret from me?' I wondered. We'd shared each other, shared our thoughts and fears and hopes, as close as two people could be. But Eden was turning out to be someone different than the man I thought I knew. Well, no matter, I decided; I would return to Nyanga and tell them there was no possibility of tearing up Mapu to recover Tree-stone, nor would there be any Amaia built.

If what Kuthula said was true, there would be little chance of saving my world, but I knew I needed to try. At the time I truly believed there was still hope, if only Eden's plans were put on hold. Maybe Kuthula was wrong when he said my world was as doomed as those past, I thought. Maybe we could change, learn more about Viria and use that knowledge to create a world where everyone is living to her fullest possible positivity. I mulled these things over in my head as Mapu shrank in the distance. The journey back to Kurrurbun was a long one but it gave me time to reflect. Many cycles[1] had passed since I left Nyanga and I was looking forward to returning home. But I did not need to be home to realize that my world had already drastically changed in my absence.

Not but a cycle away from Mapu, I noticed a great dust-cloud in the distance in a place that had previously been flat, unarable ground. I approached to investigate and saw whole sections of land were skinned, layer by layer, exposing the innards of the planet, like the organs of a corpse laid bare. Yawning pits steamed in fits of distemper, breath-clouds wheezing against the air's chill. A potent black liquid seeped from the wounds and in some places glowed orange with fire. As I traveled closer to Kurrurbun I saw more of the same devastation; holes in the earth, plant life torn up and discarded, complete destruction of the land. 'They've started without me,' I thought.

After some time traveling I saw the city of Kurrurbun. But there was something different. I could see the Beltway was still, which was odd because the Beltway was supposed to run continuously. I also noticed that there were no people conducting their daily affairs. When I pulled my transport astride the main entrance to Kurrurbun I realized the city was deserted. Abandoned. I glided through empty streets and stopped at the Governor's mansion, which was also deserted. What was the meaning of this? Had destruction come while I was away?

I charged my transport and raced from that place to Nyanga, which was cycles away but where I was sure to find the answers I sought. When I reached Nyanga I was surprised to find a different city than the one I left. The city itself was not deserted as Kurrurbun was, quite the opposite in fact. Dominating the skyline was a massive tower, round and tall as the sky itself, spewing clouds[2] into the air. The dense fog created by the tower hung over the city like a blanket, but was not thick enough to hide the numerous new dwellings that had been constructed during my short absence. Those dwellings were like nothing I'd ever seen before, stretching higher and higher into the sky, with no indication they were nearing completion.

I glided slowly past the construction areas and was immediately recognized. The workers stopped what they were doing and shouted to me, thanking me for Amaia. "Our King approaches!" they shouted as I slowed my vehicle, "You have given us a bliss we never thought possible!" I stopped and got out, approaching the workers. They abandoned their tools and rushed to greet me. I saw that, although incomplete, the dwellings were made completely of metal and already rose high enough to touch the sky. There was light radiating from every portion of the buildings and it was clear the completed areas were already inhabited.

"What are these dwellings you are constructing?" I asked the People, who had formed a circle around me and my transport. One man answered joyfully, "The King jokes with us. We are to be made fools today!" The crowd looked at me and laughed, as if my question was meant to be comedy.

But I was not amused. I reiterated, "People, you must tell me now, why are you constructing these buildings, and what gives you the power to do so?" Even as the words escaped my lips I knew the answer. The crowd quieted and another worker answered, this time solemnly, "Why, my King, it is by your decree and your generous gift of limitless power that we build these, our new homes. People from all Regions are flocking here to Nyanga to live in peace and comfort, as you have promised, to drink the reward of Amaia and live like Nobles." The People beamed at me, a strange disconnect gleamed in their eyes. Where had I seen that look before?

So it is done, I thought. Eden had built Amaia in my absence. I continued to question the People, "And why are people leaving their home Regions to come here?"

"You have told us, my King, that while construction on Amaia is being finished across the land, all who like may stay here and taste the blessing of limitless power. Amaia has already been built in four other Regions, so the People are already enjoying their new life. But we have all come to live here together in Nyanga. It is to be the largest and most luxurious city of all and the capital of Mokor[3], our united kingdom. This was your vision for us, for Amaia. As you said, the closer together we live the more comforts we may enjoy and the more unified as a world we will become. These were your words, my King."

"Mokor? Who gave the city that name, and who is funding the construction of Amaia?"

The People had lost their amused grins, which dropped into wrinkles of confusion. "Why, you named Mokor, my King. And we have volunteered all our units to complete your plan for the world, just as you have asked us to do. You said if we gave all our collection to Amaia, we would live without them and have everything we ever wanted." They stared at me, faces frozen in a confused ecstasy, their eyes glistening with desire.

I was horrified by my name being used while I was away, and more so at the product of that deceit. But for the sake of the People I hid my fears and answered in the best way possible. "Right you are. Continue with your good work and we shall live together in peace and comfort." The People let out a cheer and ran back to their work. I stood for a moment and looked at the work site. There were huge tanks, the likes of which I'd never seen before, situated randomly around the buildings, equipped to hold what looked like some type of liquid. Workers, every so often, approached these tanks and filled portable containers, took a long drink, and then rushed back to their work, seemingly invigorated. These buildings were constructed in little time, I thought, and showed no signs of completion. I knew then there was only one person who could help me, who could explain this mess. I had to find Eden.

I raced to the Governor's mansion, which, after unifying the Regions, had become the place where all government affairs were conducted. Eden was sure to be there. I found the mansion just as I'd left it, with one exception. Immediately behind the garden rose the base of the massive Amaia tower, casting a shadow that covered the once beautiful grounds, its mouth high above billowing white plumes of stifling smoke into the air. I burst through the doors to the palace and ran to the Governor's rooms. There I found Eden, just as I suspected.

It seemed that while I was gone he'd transformed the Governor's rooms into his own personal pleasure palace. People I recognized as Nobles languished in the shadows, reclined on couches, or simply lay prostrate on the floor. The same tanks I saw at the construction site were scattered throughout the palace, spewing liquid into cups or on the ground. Those who saw me had the same detached look, but they were farther gone than the workers. They laughed as I approached, hailing me as King and inviting me to drink with them.

I saw machines everywhere, strewn about the rooms, moving busily to bring more liquid to whomever desired. As I stood in horror I heard a Noble yelling to bring more drink. A machine appeared a moment later with the man's request. And there was Eden in the midst of the scene, lying naked on an elevated platform covered in pillows, smoking from a large pipe, surrounded by numerous disrobed women and men. All were in various stages of entwinement, some tending to Eden, others to whoever stranger happened to cross their path. Eden casually looked up from his harem and saw me standing at the center of the room, staring at him incredulously, tears streaking my dirty face. He smiled and rose from his pillows, moved a few people aside and found his robes.

"It is good to see you back, my King," Eden said as he approached me, pulling his garments around his naked body.

"What is this, Eden?" I asked, disbelief in my voice.

"This is our dream, yours and mine. This is merely the beginning of what Amaia can do for us. Come, let me show you." He grabbed my arm and gently began to pull me toward the orgy.

"Eden, I don't want any part of this!" I screamed, pulling away from his grip. Calming my voice, I continued.

"I've just returned from the Forgotten Land and have urgent news. We must stop building Amaia. We cannot afford this type of decadence. You of all people should know this; you are Tlinee."

At the mention of this word Eden's eyes narrowed. "Yes, I see from the filthy sand covering your feet you have visited the Forgotten Land, or is it Mapu to you now? Of course they mentioned their most famous son, the son who refused to wallow in the dirt like the rest of them, the son who would not worship a mound of filth called a mountain or give reverence to the children's stories they tell." His eyes narrowed and his voice became harsh, sarcastic. I was beginning to realize that Eden had not been truthful with me when we met, that he had a much darker[4] side to him. Unfortunately, I knew it was too late.

"They probably told you some worthless tale of invisible particles that people breath in and out that are supposed to make you feel good, right?" Eden said. I agreed they did. "And they also told you that the earth was preparing itself to purge an excess of these particles and that building Amaia would mean only certain doom for our world, yes?"

"Yes, Eden, they told me this," I said sadly, dropping my head to my chest. I knew it was beyond hope. Eden's voice revealed all.

"Well, take it from me, they are wrong," Eden said, this time putting his arms around me. I shook free and pushed him away.

My voice quivered as I spoke, "You told people it was by my command that Amaia be built, that the Forgotten Land was to be destroyed. I never wanted this! I left here on a mission of peace with the best intentions of the People in mind and I come back to this?" I said, pointing to the excess around us.

"Please, calm yourself woman. It's just like your kind

150

to let emotion overwhelm clear thought," he said, taunting me.

I answered, "Yes, Eden, I am a woman, but I am also your King. I feel deep emotion right now but my thoughts are as clear as they've ever been. I don't need to be a man to see that what you've done here is wrong. You betrayed your King, you've brought calamity to a civilization of innocents and you've lied to those you love."

"Those I love?" he laughed. "I used you, woman; love has nothing to do with it."

"So our time spent together was worthless to you?"

"I wouldn't say our time together was worthless. It was not always tedious. In fact there were moments it was mildly enjoyable. But it was not love, rather a means to an end. And trust me, if you weren't so influential with the People I would never have joined with the likes of you; these of your kind are much more to my liking," he said, gesturing to the nude female bodies writhing on the floor around us, senses enraptured in some ecstatic trance.

I spat in his face at the sound of his words, more hurt than angry. He slowly wiped the dripping moisture and grinned at me. "Not the worst fluid I've had in my face today."

"You disgust me, Eden."

He shook his head and waved his fingers at me. "You have spent too much time with those savages. They have distorted your perspective." He yelled for a machine to bring him an intoxicant. "Here, drink this, my old companion," he said offering a cup filled with a foul smelling, thick dark liquid.

"This again?" I asked, remembering the scent from our first meeting in Governor Hiru's garden. "Eden, what is this stuff?"

His voice lifted as if to proclaim a knowledge greater than any ever spoken. "This is the solution to every problem you have, the cure for every ailment your body suffers, and for you and your followers the divine blood of Aigonz Itself!" A wan cheer of agreement rose from the revelers.

I looked around at the Nobles and concubines that littered the Governor's rooms, the spectacle making it clear they'd lost all self-control. Some vomited black liquid violently in the corners, only to demand another cup. Others poured the drink down each other's throats, sending it gushing in torrents from their mouths and streaming down their faces, their bodies erupting in screams of ecstasy before returning to their reckless sensual passions.

I handed the cup back to Eden, "I do not want any of this foul concoction. Is this what you are using Amaia for, to make this awful stuff?" I asked.

"Not only for this, though Amaia has made producing it much easier," he said, downing the entire cup, excess dripping from his chin, in the light the color of blood. "Before Amaia, this single cup would take more energy to create than most could spare. But now I am manufacturing it by the barrel, enough for everyone on earth to enjoy, free of charge. The only cost is the supply of Tree-stone, which continues to arrive." Eden's eyes gleamed with intoxication. But it was more than that. He was overwhelmed with his own power.

I grabbed his arms and looked up into his eyes, "Eden, I am the King. You can not do these things in my name. I never would have approved of this. Amaia will be dismantled!"

Eden pushed me away and spit at my feet, "You fool!" he shouted. "You are no King. You are my puppet, my dog that I lead as a show. Your Kingship was a lie from the beginning, devised by the Governors and me and executed flawlessly. The People would never have listened to me; they are so stupid they never would have agreed to let me take control, to give to them the comforts they need," he taunted. "But for some reason they love you. They follow you blindly, hang on your words, obey your commands, all because of your belief in a god that hides from Its followers. So we told the People what they should want and then they demanded it. You see how easy it is? But you couldn't see through that, wise Prophet."

He was sneering at me now, his eyes wild with fury. "And do you remember your victory at our little debate? I told the Governors to rule in your favor no matter what the evidence suggested. You're a fraud, a simple-minded dolt and you never should have issued a challenge. You're no different from the savages that gave birth to me! You put your belief in an invisible power that does nothing but make demands then rolls over and dies when hardship arises. Aigonz, Viria, it's all the same thing, a lie, an ancient story from a time of primitive minds."

Eden grabbed me by the arm and pulled me outside, facing the massive white tower. "This," he said, pointing up at the thing, "this is real power. This is not an invisible god, this is not tiny pieces of positive and negative garbage, this is something we can rely upon to improve our lives! This is Amaia! This is the future of the earth, the greatest power the earth has ever seen. Look around you. Already have we constructed buildings to house all the People of the earth. Look in the distance, can you see them coming?" Eden said, pointing across the distant landscape. He was right. I saw, coursing from the outskirts, thousands upon thousands of people streaming into Nyanga, children, families, elderly, walking into the city. As I was taking in the scene I noticed the cages were no longer swinging above the city square.

"Eden, where are the cages? The criminals?"

He laughed and said, "We no longer need cages. The drink produced by Amaia is more than enough to keep everyone calm who was not before. Even if there are a few mishaps, they will be quickly forgotten. Vouchers, units, they're all worthless now; the People have surrendered their collections and are living as Nobles. And above all, here for us to enjoy—peace, as you promised, my Lord. Another cup!" he yelled. As he said this a machine appeared, its glistening metal arm offering a fresh drink. "You see," he laughed, coughing and choking as he gulped every drop, "pure, instant pleasure. This is what you have given the world. You made good on your word to them and I on my word to you." Eden threw his head back and laughed loud and long.

I was horrified by his words. He had given me all the credit for this atrocity. It was true we promised the People all the things Eden said but it wasn't supposed to happen this way. Intoxicated people walked past us shouting words of praise. "Thank Aigonz for you, my King! My pain has been released!" shouted one woman, gulping her liquid down and shouting for another. "I feel nothing, my King, and I have you to thank!" screamed another, a tremendous smile around her cracked, bleeding lips, her eyes large as moons.

"There, you see?" Eden said. "You are now their savior[6], their goddess, just like you wanted. You have delivered them from evil."

Tears ran down my face. I looked around at my people, who had before been so strong, so innocent, now wallowing in the dirt, writhing in the false pleasure provided by Eden's machine.

"Eden, why did you do this?" I pleaded.

"What have I done but fulfill your destiny?" he said. "You were destined to help me realize my vision, a unified world. You see, the Tlinee thought my ideas were useless, that I was distracting myself from Reality. But I have created a world the Tlinee only tell stories about. Peace, equality, plenty for everyone, this is the reality power can create." He began to snarl, "I showed them all these things are attainable through Science, not their invisible world with invisible things that control my life."

It was clear to me now that this was a personal war Eden was waging with his past. I hung my head knowing I'd helped him achieve his goal to defy his ancestry, to fight their ideology, and to spite those who loved him.

"Don't feel too bad, my King," Eden said, a sarcastic pity in his voice. "You were merely doing your duty, yes? It was your duty to listen to me, to be deceived by me, and now it is your duty to indulge as the rest of us will. Unlimited power, unlimited pleasure is at your disposal, my companion." Eden placed his hand to his head and bent low before me. I knew that hope was lost. Kuthula was right, this world would end.

"Don't try to stop this; the time for that is long past," sneered Eden, his voice like poison in my ears. "You have created this world and now you must live in it."

"No!" I screamed. "NO!" I pushed him and rushed past, running blindly away from Amaia into a thick crowd of people. Eden's drink was available everywhere I turned, borne by the legions of machines serving them. I looked around me and realized massive tanks of the stuff rose high off the ground, signifying an endless supply was on hand. People lay in the streets, some still alive, others covered in bugs, birds picking at their lifeless flesh. The streets flowed with every vile excrement a human is capable of producing. Children splashed in the gathering pools, themselves overwhelmed by Eden's powerful drink.

However, children will forever be children, and even in their inebriated state they played children's games. Holding hands, they danced in a circle, reciting the familiar rhyme and its simple melody. "Through time and space and spinning dust, its spectral glow for each of us, from churning froth to parched tongue, comes certainly for everyone, an ever less-forgiving friend, come quickly now, for me, the end." Over and over they sang, until their voices squeaked from exhaustion. They danced until they collapsed into the piles of filth lining the streets. And although all saw the damage being done to their world, no one cared. The only concern the People had was keeping their cups full.

I finally understood what Kuthula meant. What little positive was available was being consumed and used up. All that was left was negative, which had nowhere to go. This is when I heard the rumbling come from deep within Amaia. I shoved my way through the revelers toward my transport. This was the end, I thought. The earth was about to purge negative and all would perish. I roared away from Nyanga as quickly as my transport would take me and headed back toward Mapu and the chamber where I would spend these, my final days.

Segment 11

The Beginning

11

The return journey to Mapu seemed like a dream, so shaken was I from all that had just happened. I cried for most of the trip, not because of my own plight, which I was all too aware of, but for the People, who were innocent. It was not their fault, it was mine. They trusted me and I betrayed them. But crying for my world will not help them, I told myself. I knew I must face my final duty, and by the time I reached Mapu I was prepared for death.

But when I arrived at the village, I did not find it in the same condition it was in just a few cycles before. Most of the dwellings had been dismantled and those that still stood were being taken down hastily. I asked the villagers why they were leaving Mapu and they told me it was the order of Kuthula that all leave and flee to the east, where a new land awaited them. I needed to find Kuthula, to speak with him about what had happened. I rushed to his hut to find it gone, along with all those that had been built around it. I stood dejected and confused, wondering what to do next, when I heard a voice behind me, flowing like water, bubbling with life. I recognized that voice.

"I knew you would return." I turned to see Kuthula leaning on his cane, a broad smile sweeping across his ancient face.

"I owe you much, friend," I muttered, fighting back both fear and relief.

He walked up to me and embraced me, pulling me close to him. "The end is here, madame Prophet," he whispered. "My people and I are retreating to a land much like Mapu, where we will wait, through the next ice-period, so our progeny may greet the new age." Kuthula released me and stooped to the ground, picking up a stack of matrices and inscribing instruments I'd failed to notice. He took my arm and handed me the bundle. "You know where we must go," he said.

I dropped my head. "Yes, I know," I managed. The tumult of my experiences suddenly gave way to fear as I was struck by the reality of what lay before me. Tears trickled from my eyes as I fought to remain dignified and courageous.

"Do not be afraid," said Kuthula as we began to walk out of the deserted village toward the river. "After all, your final duty might not be to save your own age, but one that comes after."

I began to sob. Through my tears I choked out a question that was weighing heavy on my heart. "Kuthula, why does Aigonz allow this to happen, all the suffering and sadness? It told me It only wanted good for the people of earth, yet It punishes the innocent."

"This is the Aigonz you know, Prophet," answered Kuthula. "But there are many other forms Aigonz may take, as many as there are humans walking on the land."

"What is Aigonz to you, then, and to the Tlinee?" I sniffed.

Kuthula laughed softly and said, "Aigonz is whatever a person needs It to be. Some need It to be a warlord, and so it appears. Some need it to be a peacemaker, and so it appears. Some need Aigonz to cause them suffering, and It obliges, while some need Aigonz to bring meaning and so It does."

I was not satisfied so I pressed further. "But what is Aigonz to you? What does Kuthula need Aigonz to be?"

"I need Aigonz to be nothing and everything, unknowable yet clear as ice, out of reach but in the palm of my hand. I need Aigonz to be the dirt of the ground and the space between the stars, to be motion and stasis, positive and negative, good and evil. I can make no claims about Aigonz but still look to It to explain everything that needs explaining. Edensaw needed Aigonz as an adversary, you need It as a companion. This is the nature of Aigonz. This is the truth."

I stared at the ground and questioned him no more as we walked slowly and in silence. We crossed the river and continued out of the forest toward the field and the stone walls that surrounded the entrance to my tomb, the underground chamber. As we approached our destination my mind raced with possibilities. Maybe there was still a way to avoid this, to save the world. I could go with the Tlinee to their new land, live with them until time enough had passed to return and salvage what was left of my world. But as I was thinking this, the earth beneath us began shaking violently. Kuthula gripped my arm as we were both thrown to the ground by its power.

When the tremor subsided Kuthula and I rose. I could smell the winds carrying the scent of fire toward us, an oppressive musk commingled with metal and flesh. The stench clung to me, making my stomach sick from the smell of my own clothes. He pointed to the distance, toward my homeland. "See, the end of an age is upon us," he said quietly. In the distance I could see huge walls of smoke blotting out the horizon. "The first purging has begun." I bowed my head in agreement. We watched for a moment as black clouds rolled closer to Mapu, choking the light of the sun. The clouds boiled with fire and I could see orange sparkling inside them and on the ground beneath.

"The earth is burning. Your cities have been destroyed, decimated, drowned in fire," Kuthula said gravely.

"Will the Tlinee have time to travel to their new land?" I asked.

"Yes, we will survive as we have countless times before. Once we are there we can only wait for the ice to come, which it surely will."

Another quake, more violent than the last, sent us flying across the ground. "We must part ways, you and me," he said as we picked ourselves up once more. "The earth will very soon rip apart. Molten rock will burst from great fissures in the ground and the air will become poisonous for us to breathe."

It was finally the end. I let go a deep breath and patted the bundle Kuthula gave me. "I am ready."

We walked to the stairs and began to descend. I could hear rumblings in the distance as we journeyed farther into the blackness. Kuthula pulled from his robes a flint and some cloth. He wrapped the cloth around his cane and struck the stone on the wall. The cloth instantly ignited, revealing a stark white tunnel coated on all sides by the same unusual substance used to create the stairs. Kuthula took my arm for the last time and said, "Now we walk to the end, she and I."

We descended the stairs, which took us into a large tunnel. I could hear the report of explosions, rumbling through the earth but shaking the tunnel very little. "This place will survive to see another age," Kuthula mused as we approached the end of the tunnel. The light from his torch revealed a yawning doorway. The door had been removed and propped against a wall. I separated from Kuthula and inspected the door.

"How are we to put this in place?" I asked, trying to move it. It would not budge, even under my best effort.

"I will put the door where it needs to be," he answered knowingly. "Come now, there is no more time to spare." Kuthula gestured to the room behind the entranceway and, leaving the door behind, I entered the chamber. The torch revealed a rather unremarkable room with no decorations or furnishings inside. Only dust. I started to walk around the room but immediately choked on the flakes stirred up by my footsteps.

"What is all this doing here?" I asked.

Kuthula looked me straight in the eye and said very seriously, "Do not concern yourself with the contents of this chamber." He pointed to the bundle under my arm. "Only write. Do not become distracted, do not become discouraged. Consider this your most important, honorable, and sacred duty."

He stood on the other side of the entranceway, next to the door. He pulled his torch from my view and I was suddenly enveloped in complete darkness. All I could see was Kuthula looking back at me from outside, his body stooped in reverence. He held the torch high above his head and bowed to me, his chin trembling, tears dripping from his face.

"You have accomplished good, dutiful servant." His shaking voice echoed through the white hall. "This is not your end, but a new beginning."

Then the light from his torch began to disappear as the door, untouched, as though lifted by invisible giants, moved from its resting place and slowly made its way toward the opening. I rushed to the entrance and touched the door as it slowly pushed me back into the chamber. Kuthula's light blinked from sight and I felt the door come to rest in its proper place, sealing me in for the rest of my days. I crumpled to the ground and wept, coughing from the dust that hung in the air. After a few moments, I began to write, using my hands to see in the dark.

As I've been writing the chamber has shaken, sometimes violently, and I hear increasingly more rumbles through the earth. My strength is gone and I can barely force the effort to press these final words. I am ready to die. But my story has not been lost because you've read it. It has survived to see another age, your age. So tell me—how will your age end? How will your [...].

Appendix 1

The Discovery of the Manuscript

What precedes these appendices is a text unlike any other. It is not an invention, not a piece of literary inspiration. Rather, it appears to be an historical record of a civilization here on earth, a civilization that existed in the past and ended under tragic circumstances. I have spent the better half of my life translating this, alone and in secret, for what it contains must be presented with absolute certainty in my translational accuracy.

It is likely I will never know who wrote it. I haven't the slightest proof as to when or where it was written. All I have is a manuscript, presented in a previously unknown language, recounting the devastation of a people, a society, a world. Because of the importance of this task, I have abandoned what was a promising career in academia. I resigned my positions, refused subsequent offers of employment, and have not published in over thirty years.

It is important that you understand exactly the context in which the manuscript came to be in my possession, so I will use this appendix as an opportunity to recount the event. In the fall of 1977, I was enjoying an extended adjunct at a prominent university in the New England region of the United States, lecturing in Central American Religion and teaching an advanced course on translational theory and method. I am an archaeological linguist by trade and have an affinity for ancient and logographic writing systems. My interests led me to a love of the Maya culture, and so I made it my life's work to gain an intimate familiarity with Mayan language and glyphs. There was a time when scholars had no way of translating Mayan glyphs, as that system of writing had become extinct and no foundation existed from which to begin. Around the time I was entering my graduate studies, the Mayan language was beginning to be understood but was not yet readable by any standard. During the course of achieving my degrees, I worked with the finest in the field and contributed not a little to the breakthroughs that followed. As a result, I was able to achieve an intimate familiarity with the process of deciphering logographic writing systems, a skill which has been of monumental importance in translating the text at hand.

In 1977 I was still quite a young man, and had many professional acquaintances around the world. One such was a brilliant scholar, Benjamin Kuziwula Bahlah, an expert in the study of indigenous East African religion and magic. Ben had been involved with an archaeological team digging near the city of Axum, an ancient city in the Tigrinya region of northern Ethiopia. But research halted and scholars were forced to evacuate the dig when, upon the political ousting of Heili Selazi, the region was plunged into horrible civil war. Benjamin, being a native of Ethiopia, was compelled to stay and resided for a short time with a tribe of Tigrinya people in the hills surrounding ruins of the famed temple at Yeha.

I returned to my office one day to discover an envelope from Benjamin. Inside were a few pages of names, addresses, and phone numbers, as well as an airplane ticket and a letter from him. It is from this letter I now quote: "It is important that you come to Ethiopia. There is research to be done here that requires your expertise. But, you must know, the area is involved in a civil war, so travel only through the contacts I've provided. Please, you must come to see me. Take extreme care as these are dangerous times." It was an odd letter to receive and not like Ben to be so cryptic, much less to make demands. But this was, in effect, more than a request from my friend, it was a plea. This is important, I reasoned, and decided Ben's request must be taken very seriously.

Despite my comparatively few years of involvement, I had grown disinterested in the life of academia. As coincidence would have it, the courses I taught had just ended, so it was with no hesitation that I made arrangements to begin a journey to Africa. My flight took almost four days of transfers and layovers, but soon enough the sprawling African countryside stretched before me as my small prop-plane bounced to earth, jostling above the craterous dirt landing strip beneath. As we taxied I recognized Benjamin climbing out of a Jeep so covered in mud, it could have been any color underneath. I stepped off the plane and greeted him as he grabbed my shoulders and smiled.

Benjamin had at times a booming voice and he welcomed me warmly, his English bearing the beautiful African accent accentuating his high degree of scholarship. We exchanged pleasantries and climbed into his vehicle, bounding away from the landing site and into the countryside. After driving for nearly an hour, Ben slowed the Jeep to a stop and pointed to the hills on our right. "Look! See the Lion's head carved into the mountain? This signals we have reached our destination."

I turned in the direction he was pointing and saw at first only rolling hills, each to my eyes the same as the other. "There, see the eastern face of that hill. The rocky outcropping is the lion in profile," Ben insisted, pointing toward what still looked like a desert of rock and pygmy plants. Then I saw it. Sure enough, jutting from the eastern slope of one of the hills was a rounded figure, sloping into a squat snout, now obviously the shape of a lion's head. The hill was no more than 500 meters high and sparsely covered in green and brown shrubbery, as was the head itself. The surrounding countryside was much the same—very brown, dry dirt, rocky, with struggling vegetation dotting the landscape.

Ben started the Jeep moving and turned off the road,

laboring forward against the inhospitable terrain to the foot of the hill, the lion's head looming above and then behind as we continued forward. We continued past a grouping of shrubs in a small valley at the foot of two large hills, perhaps 1200 meters from the lion's head marker, stopped and turned off the car. I remember looking around as we got out of the vehicle and thinking what an unremarkable place it seemed. I had been all over the world and seen places people consider noteworthy, but this spot was unlike any of those. There were no pyramids here, no stellae, not a trace of civilization, past, present, or future, not a single burial mound to explore. So I couldn't help wondering, what makes this place so special?

As I stood surveying the landscape, Ben opened the hatch and produced two shovels, one of which he gave to me. "Buried treasure?" I quipped. "Perhaps," he sighed, and urged me forward. "See that area where there is smooth sand, no rocks or vegetation?" he said. We walked over and stood in the area Ben indicated. "Now start digging. I'm not entirely sure where the door is, only that it is in this area. It has been years since I've been here."

We began sifting with our shovels, moving the sandy dirt here and there. "We're looking for a group of large wooden planks bound together to form a door," Ben yelled, "as one may have to a cellar. At the head of this door is a large brass ring. We must locate the door and clear the area in order to open it." After a moment of digging I felt my shovel rebound against an unseen surface and heard the loud clank of metal striking metal. I stopped digging and turned to see Ben kneeling in the dirt, clearing a small area with his hands. Sure enough, in a shallow hole he made I could see the outline of a semi-circle, shining faintly in the sunlight. He cleared the dirt and pulled the ring up to reveal a sturdy brass fixture holding it in place, bolted to wooden panels. "We must clear the door," Ben said, standing and picking up his shovel.

With some effort we were able to move the dirt aside to reveal the doorway. I stood back and took a long look at what turned out to be a rather interesting archaeological find. The doorway had a rectangular metal frame, roughly 3 meters wide and 5 long, with 2 large hinges in the middle. Inside this frame lay carefully constructed wooden planks, roughly hewn, and still maintaining their original character. Despite its age, this wooden anomaly was very sturdy and I felt no anxiety standing on top and studying the craftsmanship.

We stood side by side, admiring the spectacle before our eyes. "Wow, that's amazing!" I said. "What a great site! But Ben, what's it doing *here*?"

Ben turned from the door, "This is a remnant left by the 16th century Portuguese explorer Francisco Alvares. He was the first outside of the Tigrinya to know about this spot. But you must keep in mind, this doorway is the only thing connecting Alvarez to this place. What lies beneath the door is the real treasure."

"So why hasn't anyone come looking for this treasure in 400 years? Surely this site has been documented."

"Alvares is considered an unreliable historian, having frequently been caught exaggerating the truth. But be sure, the value of this treasure cannot be measured with money, nor can it be exchanged for goods or services. It is a treasure to humanity, a long forgotten relic from our past, here to show us the future." Ben's eyes shone as spoke, the brilliant Ethiopian sun setting at his back.

He continued, "It was because of his reputation for embellishment that his tale of a mysterious underground chamber deep in the countryside of Ethiopia was ignored by historians and colleagues and disappeared from record. Plus, this area is so remote that even if someone did believe Alvares had found something it would be next to impossible to find. Alvares left almost no record of this place, so angered was he that no one believed his story."

"A mysterious underground chamber? That's the treasure?"

"Well, that…and what was found within it," Ben said, a grin spreading across his face.

"Alvares found something?" I pressed.

"No, Alvares only found an empty chamber. The contents of the chamber has been a carefully guarded secret for millennia, I have been told."

I was amazed. "Millennia? *Thousands* of years? That's pretty old."

"It's almost impossible to estimate, so unusual is its construction." Ben clapped me on the back, "But why talk any further when I can show you." He bent down and grabbed the ring. "Get a good grip and pull with me." Despite its surprising weight, we had no trouble hoisting the door open, sending it crashing down on the opposite side. Where the planks once rested now gaped to reveal a staircase, made of what appeared to be concrete, descending into complete darkness.

Concrete? This shouldn't be made of concrete, I thought. The stairs were gray in color, with an obviously rough exterior. Now I was confused. The stairway had obviously been here when Alvares found the site, yet it was virtually impossible, judging from the very modern look of the stairs and the material used to make them, that they could have been created any time before the very recent past. My only conclusion was that these stairs were too modern to have been during Alvares' time.

So I asked the obvious question, "Ben, What is a set of concrete stairs doing buried in the middle of Ethiopia and how could they have been made before the 16th century? They look like they were made by a construction company for the basement of a new house." Benjamin walked over and sat down on the first step, rubbing the surface of the stair with his palm. "Come, sit, put your hand on the stairs," he beckoned. I obliged, sitting next to him on the top step.

What I thought was concrete was most decidedly not. It had the same texture as concrete but was at the same time smooth and fibrous, like it had been somehow woven into a material different than anything I'd ever put my hand on. I stooped to look closer at the surface of the stairs and the wall that grew smaller as it descended into what was still utter darkness.

"Recognize what it is yet?" Benjamin asked.

"This structure must be modern," I insisted. "It feels like...Plastic?"

Ben smiled, "These stairs are no more modern than the 16th century; I assure you, my friend, these stairs appeared to Alvarez as they appear to you now." I was taken aback for a moment at the gravity of this archeological find and remained for a moment in quiet contemplation. Benjamin put his hand on my shoulder and got up slowly, walking away from me toward the Jeep. He returned quickly with a crowbar retrieved from the truck and handed it to me. Snapping out of my abstracted state, I took the heavy metal crowbar from him and looked up.

"If it's made out of plastic then this crowbar should make a nice little dent in it," Benjamin said. "Go ahead, take a big swing and see what happens."

Excited to prove my senses wrong I stood up, reared back, and gave a mighty swing, connecting with the top step. A sharp pain in my hands and a loud crash of the tool leaping from my grip was all that resulted from my effort. That, and a large piece of metal flying errantly, metal which seconds before had been attached to the crowbar. I picked it up and stared at the torn shard, then looked at the point of impact on the stairs. Nothing. Not even a scratch. No dent, no pieces missing...no sign of damage whatsoever.

"Why did these plastic stairs just break the crowbar?" I demanded, chuckling despite myself.

"This is a material unlike any I've ever encountered," Ben said, sitting again on the top step and pulling me down next to him. "It is completely impenetrable, will never deteriorate, and cannot be destroyed. Alvares records shooting his musket at the walls, only to have the bullet ricochet back and nearly kill him, and leaving no trace or mark on the wall."

Ben continued, "It does feel like plastic and it could very well have been constructed using the same process, but it is unlike any plastic I've ever seen. The truth is, I have no idea what it is made of. All I know is that it has been here for a long time and was created using an unknown technology by a very ancient people." I sat and stared into the blackness of the descent, my moist palm caressing the strange surface.

But as I sat absorbing all I had just encountered, I was startled to hear automatic gun fire in the distance. Ben bolted to his feet and looked in all directions. "We cannot linger," he urged, worry twisting his normally soft complexion. In the excitement of the day I had forgotten where I was...a war zone in Ethiopia. He pulled a small pocket flashlight from his cargo pants and put his hand on my shoulder. "Now I will show you the rest," he smiled, and turned the light on as we descended the steps.

The staircase was completely covered with the plastic-like material, as were the walls descending into the dark. There was a ceiling above us that followed the course of the stairs, keeping a precise distance from our heads at all times. I remember becoming somewhat entranced by the repetition of the stairs and the glow of the light in a small circle, surrounded by blackness. At one point I stumbled, forcing Benjamin to lunge after me. "Careful my friend, not much farther to go now." he said, his voice echoing through the passageway.

We descended roughly fifty meters before coming to a tunnel. The floor and the entire passage was gleaming white in the light and was again flawlessly constructed. It had an impressively flat floor and, to my amazement, arched ceilings. We began slowly walking through the tunnel, our years of classrooms and offices providing little stamina for the trek.

"Someone really went to a lot of trouble to build this," I muttered, amazed that it showed no sign of damage or age. "There must have been earthquakes in the past 4000 years - something to put a crack in this stuff?"

"I have thought of this many times," Ben replied, "performed tests attempting to burn, chip, or otherwise mutilate any portion of this structure, and I must conclude this material will withstand virtually any attack, man-made or natural. The Great Rift Valley provides many fault lines to Ethiopia, and an unusually large fault runs up through this very region, causing severe earthquakes. Many locals say that when humans have abused the earth beyond repair, the ground will split and the Red Sea will make a new home here, on Ethiopian soil.

"Yet despite tectonic activity, one will find no inconsistency on, nor any penetration of this surface from the outside. The stairs, this tunnel, and the room ahead were all built to withstand any impact, resist any force, and never deteriorate. This is likely the most impenetrable structure on earth, and it resides 50 meters below Ethiopian soil." He shook his head, "It still amazes me it has survived."
His light flashed on a bulky object against the left wall with a black rectangular gape looming behind it, big enough to be a large doorway. "Look up ahead," he said breathlessly, pointing at the newly illuminated objects. "We have reached the end."

At the tunnel's end was a door, approximately four meters tall and about one and a half wide, leaning with its top-half against the wall to our left, completing a right triangle with the wall and the floor. It had been removed from what I discovered to be the entranceway to a room, its contents obscured in darkness beyond the threshold. It was a rather unremarkable door, again coated with the same material as hosted our journey thus far. The door had no handle on either side, no lock of any kind, and no hinges attaching it to the wall; it was difficult to know how the door was actually put in place. I walked up and pushed at it, attempting to judge its weight, and quickly realized this door was completely immovable.

"What kind of a doorway is built with no hinges and is too heavy to be picked up and placed into its frame?" I asked my friend.

"This doorway was put in place by the builders with the intention of never opening it. Once that block is in place, there is no way in to the room, and also no way out, at least none that I can conceive. The local people tell stories about this place but never come here; they say it is very holy and cannot be entered by humans," Ben explained, his rich accent bouncing through the stagnant, stifling air. "They tell me a great shaman removed this block and entered the room many years ago, long before white people came to Ethiopia. When the shaman emerged, he carried a manuscript he said was put there by God and entrusted to him."

"So there was actually something in here? Artifacts were found?"

"Come with me and I will explain all I know. Walk lightly; this place does not welcome visitors." He turned his light into the room and we crept over the threshold, into the chamber.

Ben's little light immediately revealed that we had entered a fairly sizable room, maybe 15 meters square, again with stark white, unblemished walls. But Ben's light also rcvealed something we hadn't seen. Somehow, although the room was completely empty, there was a layer of dust covering the entire floor of the room, tiny particles floating through the light as our footsteps disturbed their fetid slumber. "How can this be?" I asked Benjamin.

"It's a mystery I have thought about many times. My only guess is an unpleasant one. I think that this place is a tomb, one that has interred a great number of people." Ben lowered his head and softly sighed. Sadness washed over me as I realized my comfort in the United States made me forget the luxury of peace, something Benjamin and his kin deserved but rarely experienced.

"So there were once enough people in here to make all of this dust?" I asked.

"Maybe," Ben shrugged. As I looked around I knew Ben was right and I admit I became not a little ill at the thought. I considered how many must have died here to make so much dust. A hundred? A thousand? I had no way of judging at the time, all I can say is that the dust was very thick and covered the floor. Further, this mass death must have happened a long time ago, because there were no bones, no clothes, no signs of any human life. Only dust. We stood in silence for a moment, taking in the scene, and as we did the dust began to move on its own, as though stirred by the wind. It suddenly became an awful place to be, my eyes and nose filled with the horrible stuff. I put my hand over my face and looked at Ben.

"When the entrance to this place is open, air comes quickly through the tunnel," Ben said, pulling his shirt over his face and coughing. "Better to begin our return to more inviting conditions. We have seen all there is to see."

So we turned from the vault, walked quickly through the tunnel and began climbing back up the stairs, shaking off the remnants of the dust as we went. As we ascended, I noticed a pleasant breeze sweeping down the passage, providing fresh air for us even at that great depth. Of course, I reasoned, once Alvares' door was closed and covered the only air available would be what was already there. But there was a topic of much greater interest that had not yet been discussed. Benjamin began.

"As I said, there is a legend that a manuscript was found in this place, many years ago. The manuscript found in that chamber has been in the possession of the tribes for hundreds of years, uncovered as early as the third century C.E. During this time in Ethiopian history, Christianity was making a big impact on the religious ideas of native people in the region, and it is said the Ark of the Covenant came to rest in the nearby town of Axum."

"I don't think it's much of a secret that Axum boasts itself as the Ark's true resting place," I added.

"True, it is commonly accepted knowledge that the Ark has claimed a home in Axum, but this knowledge is quite false, a fact to which I can personally attest. You see, the story of the Ark residing in Axum was originally devised to distract from the real object of interest, this chamber and the manuscript it housed; what little interest this chamber managed to generate has now been dismissed as ancient myth. Even the local people don't know where this place is, they only know stories telling of its existence."

"So how did you learn about it?" I asked, puffing as we climbed the stairs still further toward the surface.

"Well, as you remember I have lived in this region for quite some time, working with the Tigrinya people, learning and recording their stories, translating for academics, and studying the obelisks in Axum."

"So the Ark isn't in St. Mary's church?" I wondered aloud.

"No. There is no such object here in Ethiopia, that I know. During my time here I have had the privilege of befriending many interesting people, one of whom acts as a priest in St. Mary's. Over the years I have gained his trust. One evening he confided in me his knowledge of an ancient manuscript that was discovered centuries earlier, a text he claimed was sent to humans by God. But he had no knowledge of its whereabouts or what message the text revealed. I dismissed his story as yet another folk tale based on superstition, but I was to find out later he was speaking the truth."

"Does it still exist, the manuscript?"

Ben smiled at me as sunlight blinked in our eyes, revealing the surface. "Ah, yes. I have held it in my hands. It is like nothing else."

We reached the top of the staircase and I immediately sat again on the first step, this time catching my breath while we continued talking. "So, if this manuscript is kept so secret, how did you get it?"

Just as those words escaped my mouth, the sound of automatic gunfire pealed through the air, this time very close by.

"We cannot stay here," said Ben, worry sweeping over his face. He looked hurriedly around and turned to me, "I will take you to my friends; there we will be safe." We slammed closed Alvares' door, picked up our shovels, and covered the entrance with dirt. "No one will find this," said Ben. "Come on, let us hurry," he said, grabbing my arm as we ran back to the Jeep.

We tore away past the lion's head mountain and back to the dirt road. Once on the road we made good speed toward Ben's friends at the Tigrinya village, the final rays of the purple sun at our backs. I saw no signs of immanent danger, but Benjamin hadn't spoken since we left. He knew all too well what was at the other end of those gunshots...death. This part of the world was, in 1977, a terrifying place to live. I was of course ignorant to the magnitude of the situation, my comfortable life in the United States afforded me that. But Ben took it very seriously, and in a few hour's time I was to find out why.

As we bounced along through the now growing darkness, I took a moment to consider what I had just seen. It was a completely displaced, plastic chamber and stairway, supposedly created ages ago, covered by a 16th century wooden door, buried in the middle of the Ethiopian countryside—and it originally contained some sort of ancient text. It all seemed very confusing at the time.

Ben was the first to break the silence, judging we were, at least temporarily, a comfortable distance from any conflict. "I was first introduced to the manuscript after working with the Tigrinya people for over ten years. I never heard even a whisper of it before then. Actually, I'm surprised it was ever shown to me."

"So how did it happen?" I asked.

"A very old woman in the village, a shaman of sorts, one day urged me to go with her into her home. She invited me to sit and asked me to wait as she went into an adjacent room, blocked from my view by a curtain. When she emerged, she held a leather box containing a stack of odd-colored papers, and on them, hand written symbols in a dark color." Ben looked over at me and smiled, the light of excitement returning to his eyes.

He continued, "The shaman handed the stack to me and asked me if I knew where it came from."

"Where?" I urged.

"I could not tell. The script was no language I had ever seen, certainly nothing from Africa in the last 4000 years, of that I am sure."

This took a moment to register, and being a language buff I was most interested in an undiscovered human language. "Are the characters Phoenician, or pictographs?

178

Hieroglyphs?"

"It was none of these," laughed Ben. "This is a language the likes of which no one in our world has ever seen. This is a language of which we have absolutely no record."

"Can you decipher them?"

"I am learning now, with the help of my shaman friend, the most basic rules of this new language…what the symbols mean, how the thoughts are structured, and how it translates into Tigrinya. She can read the text; I do not know how, but she knows this language as if it were her own. She keeps the manuscript in her residence at the village and every day she instructs me further. I have kept a detailed journal of my efforts so far and will show this to you when we arrive at the village."

I smiled to myself and rested back in the seat, dreaming of the manuscript and the fun it would be to discover its origins. Ben continued, "When the shaman began teaching me how to interpret this new language, her instructions were that once I mastered the translation I must tell the story to the world, that the time was right for me to translate the text so all people know its story. Why she said this, I am not sure"

As we jostled through the dark night I could see fires in the hills ahead. I thought them to be rather large, showing huge columns of smoke that clouded the moon and drowned out a billion glowing stars. As if he was reading my thoughts, Benjamin turned to me and said in a concerned tone, "The smoke from those fires is much too large." As we drew closer, it became obvious we had entered a very bad situation. The village was on fire. Houses of dirt and wood lay in heaps of smoldering rubble, with many others still burning uncontrolled.

"The Derg did this," Ben said, referring to a militia group that had been terrorizing the region. He stopped the Jeep and we looked from a distance. He pointed at various smoke pillars and explained what each used to be. "That was a grain house where my friends stored what little food they had. That was where I was staying, with a kind family who had adopted me as one of their own. Now they are all dead." Ben slumped quietly in his seat, and I could only sit with my head lowered in reverence. As we sat in silence, my thoughts turned to the manuscript, which I decided was certainly destroyed. Still, I reasoned, it would be worth trying to excavate the village to see if anything of the text survived.

"We must stay here," he said finally, sniffing a little but doing his best to keep his emotions in check. "We must stay in this spot tonight and you will return to the United States on the next plane out."

"But what of the manuscript, the chamber, the shaman?" I asked. "At least we can see if anything's left."

"Wait here," Ben said, and opened his door.

"But will the Derg come back? Are we safe here?" I implored.

"There's nothing here. All are dead, that was their goal. They would rather burn the food then steal it. Nothing to fear now." Benjamin hung his head, got out slowly and walked toward the village, holding a rag to his face as he disappeared behind a wall of smoke. I closed my eyes and tried to imagine a world where this horror did not exist, where people did not live in fear. Despite my best efforts to stay alert, the excitement of the day's events overcame my resolve and I fell into a deep sleep. I awoke hours later, at the earliest light of dawn, and found Ben sitting on the ground, his back resting on my door, writing furiously on a pad of paper. "I am almost finished, my friend. All of my notes were destroyed, but I remember much and will give to you all I know."

"But what good are your notes without the original text?" I asked. Ben stopped writing and reached down to the ground beside him. Through my window came his hand, holding a small stack of loose papers. I looked at them and then at Ben. "This can't be the text; it has certainly burned."

Ben looked up and grinned. "This paper cannot be burned in any fire the Derg can create. When I left you I retrieved it from the shaman's home. She was torched to death and her house was in ruin. I found these papers sitting in a pile of smoldering embers. This is the text we have come for."

They looked like nothing in my hand. The pages were the size of those from a legal pad, and were a light gray color. The texture of the paper was smooth, as if coated with a wax-like substance that would not rub off. I ran my fingers over the text and felt deep impressions the characters made in the paper, as if they were etched or impressed into the surface of the paper rather than written on top of it. As Ben said, this was a language the likes of which I had never seen. It resembled ancient Akkadian or cuneiform and did not seem to form sentences but was instead composed of pictographs that formed glyphs.

The text itself was an array of vastly foreign symbols. At first look I was put off imagining the sheer challenge of learning something so different, but the longer I looked at the symbols the more I began to notice patterns. My experience deciphering Maya glyphs made me sensitive to the importance of recognizing similarities of characters when deciphering any language. As I began to lose myself in the text, Ben reached up and rapped his knuckles on the door frame.

"You already want to solve the riddle, this much I know," he laughed, for the first time since we arrived at the village. "Let me help. Each grapheme is used to represent a sound or combination of sounds. Graphemes are combined to form a pictograph, which then is joined to other pictographs to create glyphs that express a complete thought."

"This is simply wonderful," I exclaimed, holding up

the text. "This is going to be the greatest archaeological discovery the world has ever known!"

Ben slowly labored to his feet, stiff from hours of writing. He took the manuscript from my hands and leaned into the window. "These original pages cannot be shown to anyone. This manuscript can never fall into the wrong hands. If others were allowed to view it they will attempt their own interpretations and the subtleties of which I have been made sensitive will be lost. It must be translated into a familiar language according to the manner in which I was instructed, then revealed to the people. But the first translation must be perfect. This is your job." He raised his eyebrows and stared at me solemnly, handing me the manuscript.

"What do you mean, my job? I'll help you as best I can, but you're the one who knows how to read it. I'm starting from nothing."

"I cannot read this. I have the tools to decipher the text but to attempt translation alone is beyond my capabilities. But you have the understanding, the experience in achieving such a goal. These notes will help you. It contains all the knowledge given to me by my deceased friend. I cannot continue with this project." His shoulders slumped as he turned from the Jeep, walked to a pile of cinder blocks and sat down, arms folded and chin in his chest. I opened my door and sat down beside my friend. All of a sudden I had the overwhelming feeling I'd never see him again.

"You must do this," Benjamin muttered quietly. "I must stay here in Africa, and help my Ethiopian sisters and brothers. I do not have the expertise to complete this task. That is why I called you here. Please say you will." His eyes were a brilliant red, inflamed by tears and lack of sleep.

"Of course I will, my friend," was the best I could say, and I sat on the ground next to Ben in silent grief.

Ben was quiet for a moment, but rose and regained his

composure. "We must leave now. You will be on the next plane out of Africa, with these pages carefully concealed. Here, this is as important as the text." He handed me the notepad on which he had diligently copied numerous characters and their translation in Tigrinya and in English.

"I know I made the right choice. You are the right choice." He put his hand on my shoulder and beamed. The sun began to peal over the hills as the new day awoke. "Come, you have a plane leaving in a few hours. I will take you." So we drove back the way we came, the manuscript stashed safely in my backpack.

My return is a blur, so overcome was I with emotion about the entire event. The underground room, strange, ancient manuscripts, losing contact with a friend…it was a lot to take in all at once. Looking back, as the author says, it really is a miracle that we have this text at all.

As far as the underground chamber is concerned, I couldn't find it again if I tried.

SUDAN

ERITREA

Axum
Lion's Head Mt.
Tigrina Village

DJIBOUTI

SOMALIA

ETHOPIA

KENYA

Benjamin as a graduate student

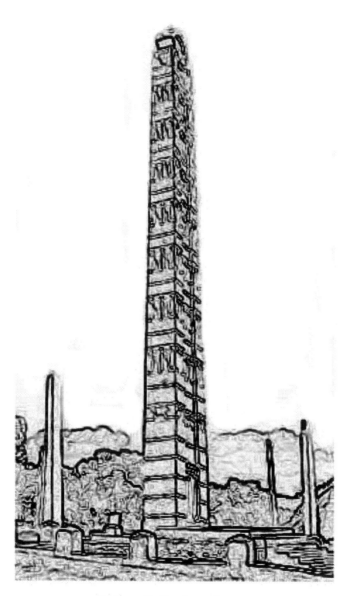

Obelisk in Axum

Church of St. Mary of Zion, Axum

Lion's Head Mountain

Appendix 2

Segment 1

1. World: This word must be understood as a sphere or domain of existential experience, a state of perception. We have a "world" in which we live, as did the author of this manuscript. The planet is the same, but our worlds are different.

2. Ages: The pictograph for this word implies a cycle of epochs, blocks of time in which occur to people distinctive events.

3. See Appendix 1 for a description of the subterranean chamber here mentioned.

4. Write: The author of this text did not "write" as we do, by creating marks on some type of matrix, but rather used a system of engraving or etching into a matrix. The matrix into which this memoir was etched looks like a cross between parchment and waxed paper, and the graphemes are an obvious bas relief. See Appendix 1 for a further description of the manuscript.

5. Prophet-King: The pictographs composing this glyph combine the symbols for "king" and "prophet" to form one unified image. The symbol for king depicts the symbol for person, predicated by the symbol for "great" or "above all," in proximity to the symbol for "population," literally "the combined force of people." The symbol I have translated as "prophet" can be read as "one who proclaims the invisible things."

6. The People: This term is used throughout the source text

to refer to a class of citizen. The glyph shows the symbol for "person" predicated by "the lesser" or "below," with "population" appearing in proximity.

7. Ice-Shelves: The glyph for this word describes massive sheets of ice that cover a large section of the earth. We are familiar with large sheets of ice at the poles of our modern planet, but it is my opinion that the author of this manuscript believed shelves of ice covered the planet, described in the text as uninhabited and not often experienced by the population.

8. Government: A transliteration may read read, "those chosen by providence to lead the population." "Providence" is one variation on the pictograph for "god," which is the basis for a number of different modes of pictograph describing this concept. In the case of "providence," "god" is modified by the grapheme "reciprocal-portion" (misaru).

9. Scribe: Because the author of this manuscript did not write on paper as we might, but rather etched into a parchment-like material, I felt it appropriate to translate this pictograph as "scribe."

10. Political: "Political" is used here out of convenience. The glyph is quite similar to that which I have translated as "government," but with a slight difference. "Government" in this context refers to a state or abstract conceptual group, while "political" adds to the symbol a modifier indicating embodied actualization of the concept. Also, "political" does not include the pictograph "providence."

11. Currency: Lit., "vouchers to be traded."

12. Vouchers: "Vouchers" was chosen as the appropriate

translation in part due to the striking similarity between the author's description of her/his currency system and our own. To use the word "money" would be appropriate, but I felt it necessary to keep our conception of money distinct from the one found in the source text.

13. Natural objects: Can also read, "Objects created from earth-dirt"

14. Cold times: "...in the cold areas and during the cold times." This phrase implies a region of the world and an era in which the temperature was much colder than when this manuscript was written. We know this world experienced large ice-shelves, a remnant perhaps of an earlier and much colder time.

15. Interest: I used "interest" here out of convenience. The glyph for this word contains the pictographs for "currency" and "in addition to the primary."

16. Wealth: Or, "a collection of units."

17. Unit: The word "unit" here can be translated as "currency," but the pictographs make it clear that units were a form of currency that had no tangible representation.

18. Earth: Lit, "The planet we have made our home."

19. Slaves: Lit., "a person who gives to another (person) his/her action by negative force."

20. Edensaw Megedagik Tassinopia: For convenience, I have shortened this name to Eden and will use this abbreviated version for the remainder of the translation, with

a few exceptions. These three words are syllabaries and a transliteration may read, "(The) glacier (lit. 'ice-mountains') (performs the action) to kill many to cause/bring about an equilibrium."

21. Evil: The glyph for evil (Yarakai) consists of the pictographs for "to find everywhere" and the syllabary "reciprocal-portion" (Misaru), modified by the grapheme for "negative," literally, "(The) negative reciprocal-portion (that can be) found everywhere."

Segment 2

1. Infant: This glyph depicts the pictograph for "person," modified by "moved into/through time," and "without memory."

2. Birth-pains: Or, "(The) woman's life-agony causing (the action of) birth."

3. Collector: This word is used throughout the text in a variety of ways. In this context, it appears as a proper name and so to distinguish it from other references to the act of collecting it has been capitalized. "Collector" should be considered a sort of profession. The text implies there was a money system through which people were able to increase their wealth.

4. Beltway: The Beltway is referenced only a few times in the text but is a fascinating study of its own. The glyph notifies us a proper name is being used, then shows the pictographs for "moving plane," "person," and "city." The ligature is then modified phonetically with the word "wrapped-around." A transliteration could read, "The moving flat-surface [(holding or keeping) people (within a) city] which wraps around."

5. Lawurl: This is the phonetic transliteration of "spirit" or "shadow."

6. Ground finder: "Ground-Finder" is a literal translation of the source glyph.

7. Illusion: Lit., "the specter of reality."

8. Death: The glyph for this word includes "person," "body," and "has (negative) motion." It is interesting that both "person"

193

and "body" appear in the same glyph, for often, linguistically, the two are indistinguishable.

9. Duty: One of the most frequently occurring words in the source text, this glyph contains the pictograph for "person," "equilibrium," and the syllabaries Kartavya, "that which must be done/accomplished," modified by "to cause/actualize." Literally this glyph could read, "(That which) a person accomplishes to cause equilibrium."

10. Hours: The use of the word "hours" is a liberty on the part of the translation, as are all increments of the passage of measured time. The source text gives references to measured time and in this instance "two hours" denotes a small portion of time taking place within a fragmented series of time-units occurring incrementally.

11. "my person had changed": The author here is referring to a change within him/her self, a sort of personality change or a change in his/her conception of him/her self.

12. Pass-time: While "pass-time" is a literal translation, it seems the author uses this term to denote an occupation.

13. Mental abnormalities: Or, "mental irregularities."

14. "I was continually uttering verses": This phrase could also read, "I was compelled (many times) to speak passages of wisdom."

15. Regions: It is claimed in the source text that the author's domain was divided into 10 different parts or entities which I have translated as "regions." It is important to note that while these regions were joined under a common rule, they

are referred to in the text as distinct.

16.   Energy: The glyph for this word contains the pictograph for "motion" or "force," and is modified by "potential." "Energy" is closely related to "power," which has a metaphysical connotation when used to describe a state of empowerment, such as the power of a King. However, "energy" is always connected to the grapheme denoting physicality, so any interpretation of "energy" as metaphysical is incorrect. There are many cases where the source text is unclear as to whether "power" of "energy" is the correct translation. In such cases I have relied upon contextual evidence to render the most accurate translation possible.

1. Passage: This word can also be translated as "passing." However, "passage" describes more accurately the tone of the glyph, which implies an incumbent action.

2. "pay the price of admission": Or, "enter at a price/cost."

3. Cages: I have inferred, using contextual evidence, that "cages" is the proper translation for this glyph. A transliteration of the glyph may read, "an apportioned space."

4. Time: This is an instance of time being referred to not in the measured sense but in a phenomenological sense. The glyph contains the pictograph for "motion," "matter," and "person" modified by "perceives" and the grapheme denoting possession unique to the subject.

5. Nyanga: A transliteration of the name of this city could read, "(The) horn of a beast."

6. "sold to the people": Lit. "given to the people at a price/cost."

7. Governor: Another morpheme that appears frequently in the source text, this word can be translated as "one whom providence has seen fit to rule (over people).

8. "create-the-Fear": "the-Fear" seems to be a condition or state of being where "fear," represented in the source text with the pictographs "person" and "emotion" modified by "negative" and "to flee from" and the grapheme "cause," is imparted on behalf of an antagonist.

9. Meters: is a liberty taken here to form for the reader a conceptual unit of measured space.

10. Soul: or "Djin."

11. "join faces with you": This phrase should be understood as a phenomenological connection between two "people-perceptions."

12. Redetrads: This morpheme has no comparable unit of measure in the goal text.

13. Dheal tree: The glyph for this morpheme has an interesting composition. In it we find a composite of the pictographs "sacred," "tree," "in the grave," and "interred in the earth." A transliteration may read, "(The) sacred tree (which is) interred in the earth (in the/a) grave." A possible translation is, "The sacred tree which is planted on top of a grave."

14. Dream-State: This should be understood as a state of being where a person has his/her perception altered while remaining among the waking world.

15. "judge the judges": Or, "pass judgment on those who pass judgment."

Segment 4

1. Debate: Or, "face to face discussion."

2. Reality: This should be understood as a state of actualization, a manifestation of the Real. I have capitalized instances of this glyph so it is not confused with "reality," a conceptual state.

3. Senses: The glyph for this morpheme includes the pictographs "person," "organs," and "receives from outside." It is interesting to note that the glyph also includes as a modifier "deception."

4. Science: Or, "a proclamation of the visible things." The actions of the referent led me to translate this pictograph as "Science." "Science" is similar in appearance to the glyph translated as "nature," literally, "the visible things."

5. Aigonz: The proper name of a primary deity in the source text, this syllabary shows another mode of the morpheme "god." In it, "god" forms a ligature with the glyph "name," which is composed of "one," a unit of measure, "actual" or "not-deceptive," and "(true) description." Thus, a transliteration could read, "(a) god whose (true) description is not deceptive."

6. Surface: A property of an object, literally "the outermost covering (of a physical object)."

7. Organ: This glyph is similar to "senses," but the modifier "deception" is replaced with "within the body."

8. Moment: This has been used throughout the target text

to refer to a number of units of measured time. I have made this generalization for the ease of the reader and because no suitable English comparisons can be made.

9. Unifier: Or, "that which brings together those that are disparate."

10. Force: Can also be translated as "motion-actualization."

11. Superhuman: the glyph for this morpheme shows the pictograph for "person" and "above (other people)," modified by "god-like."

12. Law: Or, "providential-guidance toward good."

13. "sound reason": This can also be translated as "a flawless thinking system (producing) truth."

14. Faith: A transliteration of this glyph may read, "An unencumbered belief (pertaining to some-thing)."

Segment 5

1. Reconnected: Lit., "rejoined our faces."

2. Transport: The source text refers to a vehicle of transportation for people which I have translated as "transport."

3. Threshold: "Threshold" should be understood in the context of this usage to mean the beginning or start, but also implies the entrance to a dwelling place.

4. Kurrurbun: A city appearing in the source text. This syllabary is modified by the pictographs for "city," "boundary," and "murderer."

5. Disconnection: This glyph is similar to "dream-state," but implies a state of heightened negative emotion.

6. Amaia: A machine capable of producing power. This syllabary contains a conjunction of the words "limitless" and "energy-power," modified by the glyph translated as "bearer of the finish." It is possible the author included a modifier for the benefit of our interpretation, but speculation on the prospect is moot.

7. Matter: The smallest piece of building-material, this word should be understood as both a metaphysical and a measurable unit. The glyph depicts "(a) visible thing," "to build," and "one," a unit of measure.

8. Tree-Stone: A source of power used by Amaia. Lit., "The crystalline tree-leaf."

9. Second-Life: This glyph is closely related to "resurrection,"

and "death-experience," but is modified by the action "to attain."

Segment 6

1. Quarantine: Lit., "(The) combined separation enclosures."

2. "Control devices": Pertains to some device meant to restrict a person's motion.

3. Fixed: Or, "held (to) prevent motion."

4. Yarakai Kartavya: A transliteration of "Yarakai" may read, "the negative reciprocal portion (misaru) that can be found everywhere." Kartavya may read, "that which must be done/ accomplished," or "necessary to complete."

5. Inner-Fire: Or, "(The) fire inside the body."

6. "the False Hope": The only reference to this proper name in the source text, the syllabary "hope" is modified by the pictograph "(the) negation of truth."

1. King: This glyph depicts the symbol for "person," predicated by the symbol for "held greater" or "set above others," modified by "population, or, "the combined force of people." A transliteration may read, "(The) person set above others (through) the combined force of the people."

2. Preached: This is a liberty within the target text. I based the translation of this glyph on contextual evidence of the source and the modifier "speak" and "providence."

3. God: This morpheme occurs in different modes throughout the source text and is represented here in its unmodified state. The glyph depicts the symbol for "(that which) exists," "outside matter," "(to be) esteemed," "people," and "(the act of) revelation." A detailed translation may read, "That which exists outside matter [which has been revealed to (the) people] to be esteemed."

4. Freedom: Or, "Unbinding."

5. Corpse: The glyph associated with this morpheme is an interesting one. The glyph itself is the symbol for "death," which includes the pictographs "person," "body," and "has (negative) motion." However, it is modified by a possessive and the negation of the grapheme "to possess the feminine."

6. Truth: Or, "True knowledge."

Segment 8

1. Love: Lit., "(The) surviving of many People."

2. Heart: is to be considered a metaphor.

3. Evolution: Or, "(The) changes (incurred by/of) (the collective) People."

4. Civilization: should be understood here as a condition in which people live, not a manifestation.

5. Progress: It seems the source text refers to altering the landscape as progress, as the glyph for "progress" includes "providence" and "(it is) good."

6. Consumed: Lit., "eaten to the end-state."

7. Forgotten people: "The Forgotten People" have an interesting glyph associated with their title. In the center of the image is the symbol for "group or collection of People." Surrounding the central image we find the following symbols: "to disregard from memory," "error of/in belief," "they have turned their backs," and "choose not to participate." A full translation might read, "Those People who choose (not to) participate (because of) wrong belief and so have been disregarded (to the point of) forgetting."

8. Forgotten Land: This glyph shows the symbol for "expanse on which people walk" which I translate as "land." This is modified by the pictograph "to disregard from memory" and "apart from the primary." So, a full translation would read, "An expanse (on which people walk) apart from the (primary) land which has been disregarded (to the point of)

forgetting."

9. Release (from my burden): Lit., "to let this duty lapse."

Segment 9

1. The source text is becoming increasingly more difficult to read. Glyphs are becoming disorganized and poorly inscribed, leaving but weak impressions in the matrix.

2. Blasphemous: This should be understood as "(a) person speaking against the true god."

3. Tlinee: Lit., "(The) people."

4. Eskarne: Lit., "(The) one who gives mercy."

5. Beasts/animals: These terms can be used interchangeably.

6. Pray: a difficult word to arrive at considering the symbols with which it is associated. The symbols translate as follows: "an offering of allegiance," "to make an appeal," "dwells within," "another living-space," and "the static One." From these I find the glyph can read "an offering of allegiance (in order to) make an appeal to the static One (who) dwells within another living space."

7. Sacred: Or, "(that) which the people hold in esteem."

8. Mapu: Lit., "the land on which people walk."

9. Spirits: The glyph for this morpheme shows the pictograph for "the act of motion," "outside," "matter," and "shadow."

10. "The-Tree-That-Was-Broken": Appears here as literal translation of the source syllabary.

11.   Kuthula: This syllabary is composed of the glyph for "peace," modified by the grapheme "to bring" and "to the people." Thus, a transliteration may read, "(The one) to bring peace to (the) people."

12.   Balance: also, "equilibrium."

13.   Mirror: Or, "The surface of (the other) face."

14.   Djin: The glyph for this morpheme includes "person," "body" and "inhabit," modified by the negation "outside" and the pictograph "spirit." A full translation may read, "(The) spirit-person (which) inhabits the body (on the) outside."

15.   Body: Lit., "That which conceals."

16.   Transformers: Lit., "That which creates changes in matter."

17.   Misaru: This word occurs many times in the source text, however here it appears in a unique usage. The syllabary can be translated as "reciprocal-portion" and in this context it is modified by the pictographs for "person" and "Viria." In no other place does the source text "misaru" appear in this form.

18. Ice-Period: Lit., "(The) time of ice."

1. Cycles: This glyph refers to a unit of time that has no comparable translation. It is impossible to know precisely how much time is expressed in the source text.

2. Clouds: Or., "The sky-breath."

3. Mokor: Lit., "(The) place that is asleep."

4. Darker: The glyph for this morpheme contains the pictograph "person," "light," and is modified by the grapheme "lessen."

5. Savior: Or, "(That) person who retrieves the population."

Ages – The pictograph for this word implies a cycle of epochs, blocks of time in which occur to people distinctive events.

Aigonz – The proper name of a primary deity in the source text, this syllabary shows another mode of the morpheme "god." In it, "god" forms a ligature with the glyph "name," which is composed of "one," a unit of measure, "actual" or "not-deceptive," and "(true) description." Thus, a transliteration could read, "(a) god whose (true) description is not deceptive."

Amaia – A machine capable of producing power. This syllabary contains a conjunction of the words "limitless" and "energy-power," modified by the glyph translated as "bearer of the finish." It is possible the author included a modifier for the benefit of our interpretation, but speculation on the prospect is moot.

Balance – also, "equilibrium."

Beasts/animals – These terms can be used inter-changeably.

Beltway – The Beltway is referenced only a few times in the text but is a fascinating study of its own. The glyph notifies us a proper name is being used, then shows the pictographs for "moving plane," "person," and "city." The ligature is then modified phonetically with the word "wrapped-around." A transliteration could read, "The moving flat-surface [(holding or keeping) people (within a) city] which wraps around."

Birth-pains – Or, "(The) woman's life-agony causing (the action of) birth."

Blasphemous – This should be understood as "(a) person speaking against the true god."

Body – Lit., "That which conceals."

Cages – I have inferred using contextual evidence that "cages" is the proper translation for this glyph. A transliteration of the glyph may read, "an apportioned space."

Civilization – should be understood here as a condition in which people live, not a manifestation.

Clouds – Or., "The sky-breath."

Cold times – "...in the cold areas and during the cold times." This phrase implies a region of the world and an era in which the temperature was much colder than when this manuscript was written. We know this world experienced large ice-shelves, a remnant perhaps of an earlier and much colder time.

Collector – This word is used throughout the text in a variety of ways. In this context, it appears as a proper name and so to distinguish it from other references to the act of collecting it has been capitalized. "Collector" should be considered a sort of profession. The text implies there was a money system through which people were able to increase their wealth.

Consumed – Lit., "eaten to the end-state."

"Control devices" – Pertains to some device meant to restrict a person's motion.

Corpse – The glyph associated with this morpheme is an

interesting one. The glyph itself is the symbol for "death," which includes the pictographs "person," "body," and "has (negative) motion." However, it is modified by a possessive and the negation of the grapheme "to possess the feminine."

"create-the-Fear" – "the-Fear" seems to be a condition or state of being where "fear," represented in the source text with the pictographs "person" and "emotion" modified by "negative" and "to flee from" and the grapheme "cause," is imparted on behalf of an antagonist.

Currency – Lit., "vouchers to be traded."

Cycles – This glyph refers to a unit of measured time that has no comparable translation. It is impossible to know precisely how much time is expressed in the source text.

Darker – The glyph for this morpheme contains the pictograph "person," "light," and is modified by the grapheme "lessen."

Death – The glyph for this word includes "person," "body," and "has (negative) motion." It is interesting that both "person" and "body" appear in the same glyph, for often, linguistically, the two are indistinguishable.

Debate – Or, "face to face discussion."

Dheal tree – The glyph for this morpheme has an interesting composition. In it we find a composite of the pictographs "sacred," "tree," "in the grave," and "interred in the earth." A transliteration may read, "(The) sacred tree (which is) interred in the earth (in the/a) grave." A possible translation is, "The sacred tree which is planted on top of a grave."

Disconnection – This glyph is similar to "dream-state," but implies a state of heightened negative emotion.

Djin – The glyph for this morpheme includes "person," "body" and "inhabit," modified by the negation "outside" and the pictograph "spirit." A full translation may read, "(The) spirit-person (which) inhabits the body (on the) outside."

Dream-State – This should be understood as a state of being where a person has his/her perception altered while remaining among the waking world.

Duty – One of the most frequently occurring words in the source text, this glyph contains the pictograph for "person," "equilibrium," and the syllabaries Kartavya, "that which must be done/accomplished," modified by "to cause/actualize." Literally this glyph could read, "(That which) a person accomplishes to cause equilibrium."

Earth – Lit, "The planet we have made our home."

Edensaw Megedagik Tassinopia – For convenience I have shortened this name to Eden and will use this abbreviated version for the remainder of the translation, with a few exceptions. These three words are syllabaries and a transliteration may read, "(The) glacier (lit. 'ice-mountains') (performs the action) to kill many to cause/bring about an equilibrium."

Energy – The glyph for this word contains the pictograph for "motion" or "force," and is modified by "potential." "Energy" is closely related to "power," which has a metaphysical connotation when used to describe a state of empowerment, such as the power of a King. However, "energy" is always connected to the grapheme denoting physicality, so any interpretation of "energy" as metaphysical is incorrect. There are many cases where the source text is unclear as to whether "power" or "energy" is the correct translation. In such cases I have relied upon contextual evidence to render the most accurate translation possible.

Eskarne – Lit., "(The) one who gives mercy."

Evil – The glyph for evil (Yarakai) consists of the pictographs for "to find everywhere" and the syllabary "reciprocal-portion" (Miseru), modified by the grapheme for "negative," literally, "(The) negative reciprocal-portion (that can be) found everywhere."

Evolution – Or, "(The) changes (incurred by/of) (the collective) People.

Faith – A transliteration of this glyph may read, "An unencumbered belief (pertaining to some-thing)."

Fixed – Or, "held (to) prevent motion."

Force – Can also be translated as "motion-actualization."

Forgotten People – "The Forgotten People" have an interesting glyph associated with their title. In the center of the image is the symbol for "group or collection of People." Surrounding the central image we find the following symbols: "to disregard from memory," "error of/in belief," "they have turned their backs," and "choose not to participate." A full translation might read, "Those People who choose (not to) participate (because of) wrong belief and so have been disregarded (to the point of) forgetting."

Forgotten Land – This glyph shows the symbol for "expanse on which people walk" which I translate as "land." This is modified by the pictograph "to disregard from memory" and "apart from the primary." So, a full translation would read, "An expanse (on which people walk) apart from the (primary) land which has been disregarded (to the point of) forgetting."

Freedom – Or, "Unbinding."

God – This morpheme occurs in different modes throughout the source text and is represented here in its unmodified state. The glyph depicts the symbol for "(that which) exists," "outside matter," "(to be) esteemed," "people," and "(the act of) revelation." A detailed translation may read, "That which exists outside matter [which has been revealed to (the) people] to be esteemed."

Government – A transliteration may read read, "those providence has chosen to lead the population." "Providence" is one variation on pictograph for "god," which is the basis for a number of different modes of pictograph describing this concept. In the case of "providence," "god" is modified by the grapheme "reciprocal-portion" (Miseru).

Governor – Another morpheme that appears frequently in the source text, this word can be translated as "one whom providence has seen fit to rule (over people)."

Ground finder – "Ground-Finder" is a literal translation of the source glyph.

Heart – is to be considered a metaphor

Hours – The use of the word "hours" is a liberty on the part of the translation, as are all increments of the passage of measured time. The source text gives references to measured time and in this instance "two hours" denotes a small portion of time taking place within a fragmented series of time-units occurring incrementally.

"I was continually uttering verses" – This phrase could also read, "I was compelled (many times) to speak passages of wisdom."

Ice-Period – Lit., "(The) time of ice."

Ice-Shelves – The glyph for this word describes massive sheets of ice that cover a large section of the earth. We are familiar with large sheets of ice at the poles of our modern planet, but it seems as though the author of this manuscript believed shelves of ice covered the planet the author describes as being uninhabited and not often experienced by the population.

Illusion – Lit., "the specter of reality."

Infant – This glyph depicts the pictograph for "person," modified by "moved into/through time," and "without memory."

Inner-Fire – Or, "(The) fire inside the body."

Interest – I used "interest" here out of convenience. The glyph for this word contains the pictographs for "currency" and "in addition to the primary."

"join faces with you" – This phrase should be understood as a phenomenological connection between two "people-perceptions."

"judge the judges" – Or, "pass judgment on those who pass judgment."

King – This glyph depicts the symbol for "person," predicated by the symbol for "held greater" or "set above others," modified by "population, or, "the combined force of people." A transliteration may read, "(The) person set above others (through) the combined force of the people."

Kurrurbun – A city appearing in the source text. This syllabary is modified by the pictographs for "city," "boundary," and "murderer."

Kuthula – This syllabary is composed of the glyph for "peace," modified by the grapheme "to bring" and "to the people." Thus, a transliteration may read, "(The one) to bring peace to (the) people."

Law – Or, "providential-guidance toward good."

Lawurl – This is the phonetic transliteration of "spirit" or "shadow."

Love – Lit., "(The) surviving of many people."

Mapu – Lit., "the land on which people walk."

Matter – The smallest piece of building-material, this word should be understood as both a metaphysical and a measurable unit. The glyph depicts "(a) visible thing," "to build," and "one," a unit of measure.

Mental abnormalities – Or, "mental irregularities."

Meters – is a liberty taken here to form for the reader a conceptual unit of measured space.

Mirror – Or, "The surface of (the other) face."

Misaru – This word occurs many times in the source text, however here it appears in a unique usage. The syllabary can be translated as "reciprocal-portion" and in this context it is modified by the pictographs for "person" and "Viria." In no other place does the source text "Misaru" appear in this form.

Mokor – Lit., "(The) place that is asleep."

Moments – This has been used throughout the target text to refer to a number of units of measured time. I have made this generalization for the ease of the reader and because no suitable English comparisons can be made.

"my person had changed" – The author here is referring to a change within him/her self, a sort of personality change or a change in his/her conception of him/her self.

Natural objects – Can also read, "Objects created from earth-dirt"

Nyanga – A transliteration of the name of this city could read, "(The) horn of a beast."

Organ – This glyph is similar to "senses," but the modifier "deception" is replaced with "within the body."

Passage – This word can also be translated as "passing," however "passage" describes more accurately the tone of the glyph, which implies an incumbent action.

Pass-time – While "pass-time" is a literal translation, it seems the author uses this term to denote an occupation.

"pay the price of admission" – Or, "enter at a price/cost."

People, The – This term is used throughout the source text to refer to a class of citizen. The glyph shows the symbol for "person" predicated by "the lesser" or "below," with "population" appearing in proximity.

Political – "Political" is used here out of convenience. The glyph is quite similar to that which I have translated as "government," but with a slight difference. "Government" in this context refers to a state or abstract conceptual group, while "political" adds to the symbol a modifier indicating embodied actualization of the concept. Also, "political" does not include the pictograph "providence."

Pray – a difficult word to arrive at considering the symbols with which it is associated. The symbols translate as follows: "an offering of allegiance," "to make an appeal," "dwells within," "another living-space," and "the static One." From these I find the glyph can read "an offering of allegiance (in order to) make an appeal to the static One (who) dwells within another living space."

Preached – This is a liberty within the target text. I based the translation of this glyph on contextual evidence of the source and the modifier "speak" and "providence."

Progress – It scems the source text refers to altering the landscape as progress, as the glyph for "progress" includes "providence" and "(it is) good.

Prophet-King – The pictographs composing this glyph combine the symbols for "king" and "prophet" to form one unified image. The symbol for king depicts the symbol for person, predicated by the symbol for "great" or "above all," in proximity to the symbol for "population," literally "the combined force of people." The symbol I have translated as "prophet" can be read as "one who proclaims the invisible things."

Quarantine – Lit., "(The) combined separation enclosures."

Reality – This should be understood as a state of actualization, a manifestation of the Real. I have capitalized instances of this glyph so it is not confused with "reality," a conceptual state.

Reconnected – Lit., "rejoined our faces."

Redetrad – This morpheme has no comparable unit of measure in the goal text.

Regions – It is claimed in the source text that the author's domain was divided into 10 different parts or entities which I have translated as "regions." It is important to note that while these regions were joined under a common rule, they are referred to in the text as distinct.

"release (from my burden)" – Lit., "to let this duty lapse."

Sacred – Or, "(that) which the people hold in esteem."

Savior – Or, "(That) person who retrieves the population."

Science – Or, "a proclamation of the visible things." The actions of the referent led me to translate this pictograph as "science." "Science" is similar in appearance to the glyph translated as "nature," literally, "the visible things."

Scribe – Because the author of this manuscript did not write on paper as we might, but rather etched into a parchment-like material, I felt it appropriate to translate this pictograph as "scribe."

Second-Life – This glyph is closely related to "resurrection," and "death-experience," but is modified by the action "to attain."

Senses – The glyph for this morpheme includes the pictographs "person," "organs," and "receives from outside." It is interesting to note that the glyph also includes as a modifier "deception."

Slaves – Lit., "a person who gives to another (person) his/her action by negative force."

"sold to the people" – Lit. "given to the people at a price/ cost."

Soul – or "Djin."

"sound reason" – This can also be translated as "a flawless thinking system (producing) truth."

Spirits – The glyph for this morpheme shows the pictograph for "the act of motion," "outside," "matter," and "shadow."

Superhuman – the glyph for this morpheme shows the pictograph for "person" and "above (other people)," modified by "god-like."

Surface – A property of an object, literally "the outermost covering (of a physical object)."

"the False Hope" – The only reference to this proper name in the source text, the syllabary "hope" is modified by the pictograph "(the) negation of truth."

"The-Tree-That-Was-Broken – Appears here as literal translation of the source syllabary.

Threshold – "Threshold" should be understood in the context of this usage to mean the beginning or start, but also implies the entrance to a dwelling place.

Time – This is an instance of time being referred to not in the measured sense but in a phenomenological sense. The glyph contains the pictograph for "motion," "matter," and "person" modified by "perceives" and the grapheme denoting possession unique to the subject.

Tlinee – Lit., "(The) people."

Transformers – Lit., "That which creates changes in matter."

Transport – The source text refers to a vehicle of transportation for people which I have translated as "transport."

Tree-Stone – Lit., "(The) crystalline tree-leaf."

Truth – Or, "True knowledge."

Unifier – Or, "that which brings together those that are disparate."

Unit – The word "unit" here can be translated as "currency," but the pictographs make it clear that units were a form of currency that had no tangible representation.

Vouchers – "Vouchers" was chosen as the appropriate translation in part due to the striking similarity between the author's description of her/his currency system and our own. To use the word "money" would be appropriate, but I felt it necessary to keep our conception of money distinct from the one found in the source text.

Wealth – Or, "a collection of units."

World – This word must be understood as a sphere or domain of existential experience, a state of perception. We have a "world" in which we live, as did the author of this manuscript. The planet is the same, but our worlds are different.

Yarakai Kartavya – A transliteration of "Yarakai" may read, "the negative reciprocal portion (Miseru) that can be found everywhere." Kartavya may read, "that which must be done/ accomplished," or "necessary to complete."